BROKEN TRUST

BROKEN SERIES BOOK THREE

paige press

BROKEN TRUST

BROKEN SERIES BOOK THREE

STELLA GRAY

Copyright © 2021 by Stella Gray
All rights reserved.
No part of this book may be reproduced in any form or by any electronic or mechanical means, including information storage and retrieval systems, without written permission from the author, except for the use of brief quotations in a book review.

Paige Press
Leander, TX 78641

Ebook:
ISBN: 978-1-953520-58-6

Print:
ISBN: 978-1-953520-59-3

Editing: Erica Russikoff at Erica Edits
Proofing: Michele Ficht

ALSO BY STELLA GRAY

The Zoric Series

Arranged Series

The Deal

The Secret

The Choice

Convenience Series

The Sham

The Contract

The Ruin

The Convenience Series: Books 1-3

Charade Series

The Lie

The Act

The Truth

The Bellanti Brothers

Dante

Broken Bride

Broken Vow

Broken Trust

Marco

Forbidden Bride

ABOUT THIS BOOK

You can't run from the past... or from a Bellanti.

I've always been a foolish girl.
I should have learned my lesson the first time a man betrayed me.
It hurt when Rico abandoned me. My father's deal was agony.

Dante's betrayal... it might kill me.

And there's nothing I can do.
He's not the kind of man who takes orders from his wife.
And he'll never let me leave.
There's nowhere I can go that he won't find me.

My father forced me to marry him.

Dante made me love him.

It's my turn to show them all what a Bellanti woman is…

PROLOGUE

DANTE

It's well past midnight when I enter the keypad code for the gate that secures the main entrance to the Deep Cellar.

The partially underground structure serves as a climate-controlled warehouse for the Bellanti family's personal wine collection, as well as highly select priceless vintages. This place is so off the grid, only a handful of people know of its existence—and even fewer know what else goes on down here.

The gate automatically clicks shut behind me, and I walk through the front storage room to the far back where the tunneled cellar goes deep underground. My footfalls echo on the cement floor as I traverse the short tunnel toward the dull red glow of a cigarette at the end.

It's been a while since the soundproof hidden

room has served a more devious purpose than carefully storing expensive wine, but judging by the look on Donovan's face as I approach, Armani is making up for lost time.

"Bregman's inside?" I ask, even though I already know the answer.

The man responsible for my father's death is in there. I can feel it.

Though technically, George Bregman isn't the responsible party. He's just the man who sabotaged my father's vehicle—on someone else's orders. There's more to the story, and we need to get it out of Bregman one way or another.

Hence the need for this...meeting.

Donovan drops his cigarette and crushes it under his boot, then grabs the handle of the heavy, arched wood door that muffles the sounds of what's going on inside the cellar.

"Yes, boss. Armani's...taking care of him," he says. "You want me to lend a hand, you just say the word."

"Will do."

I take a deep breath. Then I nod for him to open the door.

Donovan puts on a good show when it comes to playing the family's personal driver, but of course he's much more than that. He's loyal, discreet, and he can clean up any mess—any mess at all. It's the reason I hired him. And he hasn't let us down yet.

I make my way down another passageway, past long racks of bottles, all retrofitted to be shock absorbing and fireproof. They also keep the cellar soundproof. Which is good, because Armani is apparently doing something to Bregman that's making him scream, low and guttural. I steel myself for what I'm about to see as I round the corner.

It's not as bad as it could be. Bregman is tied to a sturdy wooden chair. Head strapped to the tall back. Arms and legs bound. Nothing I haven't seen before.

Armani stands behind him with one of Bregman's hands splayed behind his back, the wrist twisted unnaturally so most of the fingers point up. Blood has dripped onto the floor from the fingernail Bregman already lost. By the looks of it, Armani is about to remove another.

"F-f-fucking Jesus fuck!" Bregman is stuttering, sweat pouring down his face.

"Not to worry," Armani soothes, the picture of calm. "Nails grow back. Unlike balls. All things considered, I'd say it could be a lot worse. Don't you think?"

"Please, fuck, stop. Please, stop!"

Armani has the pliers clamped firmly around the nail he intends to remove, but before he can start pulling, I interrupt with, "Has he said anything yet?"

My brother stops what he's doing to look up at me. "Nothing besides 'please stop' and 'I don't know anything.' He's like a goddamn broken record."

His face has a look of pure disgust, but it's not because he detests his prisoner—it's because he hates this whole process. Armani takes no pleasure in playing torturer, despite acting every inch the hardass. It's all for show. An effort to rattle Bregman further, get him talking as quickly as possible. I know from past experience that Armani will barely eat for the next few days, that he'll brood in his office, that when it comes to his job, he'll continue doing everything in his power to avoid future interrogation sessions like this one. Cruelty doesn't come naturally to him; it never has. He's no Enzo Bellanti, and I'm glad for it.

A hum rumbles in my throat. "Maybe we should give Donovan a turn, after all. He's chomping at the bit out there."

"Oh yeah?" Armani says, playing along.

I nod. "The man brought his own tools. Not that we don't have plenty here."

Now there's a man who derives a certain relish from this kind of thing. In which case, fuck fingernails; Donovan likes playing with fire. Actual fire.

Turning to Bregman, I ask, "Do you know what a knee splitter is? You like walking, right?"

He begins to sob uncontrollably. Walking closer, I circle the chair he's tied to and get a good look at his battered face. His left eye is swollen shut, both lips split. I lean down, so I can look him in his one good eye.

"You'll answer my questions or I'll have my friend come in here and rip your balls out of your sack so he can stuff them down your throat," I tell him. "We understand each other?"

Bregman nods, breathing hard. Good. Progress.

"You're a mechanic at Sonoma Speedway, yes?"

"Yes! Yes."

"You altered Enzo Bellanti's car while he was there for one of Marco's races, yes?"

Bregman hesitates. I motion to Armani, who picks up the pliers again.

"Yes! Goddammit, yes! Please don't hurt me again," Bregman says, his voice jagged.

I wave Armani away, and he drops the pliers on a bench with a sigh, as if he's disappointed he can't use them.

Taking our prisoner's chin in my hand, I force him to look up at me with his good eye. "I want the whole story. All of it. Now."

"Okay, okay, anything you want," he says, trying

to steady his breathing. "There was a guy. He showed up at the garage one day with twenty grand in a paper bag. Said he'd give me eighty more if I made a few changes to Enzo's car so he'd have an accident."

"So he'd have an accident?" Armani repeats, his voice icy. "Or so he'd die?"

Bregman's shaking his head. "No. The guy never said a fatal accident, just enough to shake Enzo up a little."

"Liar," I say, grabbing the pliers myself and hitting him upside the head with them even as he screams and begs to be left alone.

"It's the fucking truth!" Bregman wails. "I swear. What I did to that car, it shouldn't've even made it to the freeway. It was supposed to break down before he even hit thirty-five miles an hour, thirty-five max, I swear. I never thought he'd fucking die, swear to fucking God."

"Shut up. You're babbling," I tell him, my voice full of contempt.

Armani comes up beside me and crosses his arms. "Who hired you, Bregman?"

"I don't know."

Armani's arm shoots out, lightning quick, and he backhands Bregman across the face.

"Who. Fucking. Hired you."

But Bregman's adamant. "Jesus Christ, I don't know him! I don't know. Never got his name and I never saw him again."

"How'd you get the other eighty k then?" Armani pushes.

Bregman shakes his head again. "I didn't. He never paid me the rest of the money, but I left it alone. I was too scared to try finding him."

"Bullshit." It's my turn now. I grab Bregman by the hair and wrench his head back hard. "Gimme the fucking name."

"I swear, I don't have a name!"

"You killed a man without knowing how you'd get paid for it?" Armani scoffs. "You really that fucking stupid?"

"He was gonna kill me if I didn't do it—I didn't have a choice!" Bregman whimpers pathetically.

"How was he supposed to get into contact with you?" I prod. "There had to be a way."

He hesitates, and I let go of his hair and stride toward the hall.

"Let me know when you run out of nails to pull," I call over my shoulder to Armani. "I'm fucking done with this lying sack of shit."

"No!" Bregman shouts. "Wait, please, wait!"

I turn back around, spreading my hands. Armani

has Bregman's arm twisted painfully behind his back again, and he's breathing hard.

"This is your last chance," I tell him.

"I'm not lying," Bregman insists, gasping for air. "Like I said, the old man wasn't supposed to die. The money guy sent me a few texts after the whole thing, but I never saw him again, I never got paid the rest. I swear."

"Describe this guy," Armani says. "The one who gave you the job."

"Blonde hair, light skin, tall, over six foot," Bregman blubbers, his voice pitching high with panicked desperation. "Light eyes, maybe green or blue, I don't know. Not brown, not dark. He's got a tattoo going up his neck. Antlers or spikes or something."

"You said he texted you." Bregman nods and I look at my brother. "You got his cell?"

Armani pulls out a shitty burner phone from his pocket. He powers it up and uses one of Bregman's unbloodied fingers to unlock the screen, then hands it to me.

There's no reception down here, but I don't need it to find what I'm after. I scan the messages and see texts from an overseas number, along with a photo of Marco's racing Porsche. There are instructions to tamper with Marco's car the same as Enzo's, and threats against Bergman if he chooses not to cooperate.

"How about that," I say slowly, flashing the screen at Armani before scrolling back through the older messages.

My eyes track to Bergman's. He slumps in his bindings, as if he can shy away from us. As if there's any hope of escape.

There's not.

Holding the phone, I read out loud:

Eighty k transferred conf # 20223270247210.

You'll get another 160 to fix up the Porsche before the race next week.

I let out a low whistle.

"Now that's a pretty penny," I say colly. "Over a quarter million total, right, Bregman? Enough to retire on, if you go to Mexico. I hear Ecuador's nice, too. Great beaches."

Bregman begins to whimper and twist against his bonds.

"You lied," I say with a sigh.

Bregman's eyes go wide, his face falling as realization sets in. His fate is sealed.

"One more chance, asshole. I need the name of the man who hired you," I tell him. "The name—*now*—in exchange for your life. And then you get twenty-four hours to leave the country and never come back. Because I'm feeling generous."

"More than generous," Armani says.

"I swear I don't know!" Bregman chokes out. "I swear on my life! But the money guy, it really was the tattoo guy. That's all I know!"

Armani and I look at each other. I nod.

He withdraws a Glock from his jacket and Bregman starts up with the begging again. I turn and walk back down the hall, knocking for Donovan to open the door just as a shot fires.

There's no doubt. Someone is out for the Bellanti family.

Time to circle the wagons and prepare for war.

1

FRANKIE

Miami sucks.

It's Thanksgiving week, for crying out loud. How can it still be so muggy and hot? I just showered half an hour ago and my hair and clothes are already damp with sweat again and sticking to my skin. Which means the wet spot from scrubbing vomit off the front of my red polyester uniform is going to take forever to dry before I head to work. Damn humidity.

And double damn my stomach that refuses to keep anything down.

The bathroom floor tiles are cool at least as I sit on the floor, anxiously waiting for another heave to rip through me. I have a hair dryer in one hand, plugged in and ready to dry the spot on my dress. No one wants a waitress that smells like vomit. But I don't have the strength to turn the dryer on yet. It feels better just to sit here...and wait.

My eyes track to the edge of the bathtub, but I can't bring myself to look at what's sitting there. The reason I'm going to be late to work again.

I've only managed to arrive on time twice since I started this job, and it's honestly a mystery why I haven't been fired yet. Gearing myself up to walk into the diner takes some effort. The deep-fried smells have really been getting to me. Greasy bacon, the lingering scent of browning onions, burnt coffee, tuna melts on rye. The rotten dairy stench of coffee creamer and the metallic tang of ketchup when I refill the bottles. It makes my stomach roll.

Of course, I've always had a nervous stomach when it comes to stress. But this is different.

It's been going on for a while now.

Hence the little plastic stick balanced on the edge of the tub at this very moment.

Just then, there's a loud thud against the closed bathroom door. With a groan, I scoot back and brace myself against the door. The lock is broken and it doesn't take much to push it open. A low whine sounds, followed by heavy panting from the other side.

"I don't need any help, Miggy, but thank you," I say.

My mom's huge mastiff took an immediate liking to me and barely leaves my side now. I can't go anywhere without him following me. Remembering the hair dryer, I flick it on and aim the nozzle in the crack beneath the door. For a dog that's the size of a small horse, he sure is a weenie about a lot of things. There's another whine followed by the *clip, clip, clip* of his nails on the laminate floor as he retreats. I sit there for a few minutes and turn the hair dryer onto my wet uniform. The heat feels soothing, even though I'm sweating.

Finally, I stand and unplug the hair dryer, tucking it back into the vanity drawer. I catch my reflection in the warped medicine cabinet mirror. My distorted image looks back at me. It's hard to even recognize myself. And not completely because of the funhouse mirror, either. I look haggard, the bags beneath my eyes puffy, my hair frizzy and limp.

How the fuck did I end up here?

Oh right. Selfish father. Lying husband. The ever-tightening noose of responsibility punctuated by the ever-present theme of Extremely Disappointing men in my life. It was either leave Napa or explode. So I took off in the Jag Dante's money had bought me and drove to the one place nobody would ever think to look for me—my mother's apartment in Florida.

She'd been floored to find me standing on her

doorstep, but even though we hadn't spoken since she came to my wedding in Napa, she didn't turn me away. And even better, she didn't ask a lot of questions. In fact, she hasn't asked me anything at all, perhaps assuming the worst about the state of my marriage. I'm not sure if that's good or bad, but it's typical of her not to get too invested in her children's lives. She abandoned us, after all, and never looked back.

I didn't actually intend to end up here. It just sort of happened. The only person I told was Charlie, and she'd die before telling Dante where I am. Plus, she can lie like the devil herself when she wants to... so there's no way my ex-husband will find me. If he even wanted to...

My heart lurches at the thought of him, the same way it does a hundred times a day because I can't stop thinking about him. It's miserable. But there doesn't seem to be anything I can do about it.

Stepping back from the mirror, I can't help freaking out about the way my reflection in the wavy glass makes my lower torso bulge strangely. So I look away and step over to the chipped, avocado-colored tub, lowering myself to sit on the edge. This whole apartment is like a freaking time capsule of what had to be the height of interior design in the 1960s. And the kitchen—it's all turquoise cabinets and flowered linoleum flooring and this weird spiky light fixture that I'm constantly hitting my head on. I mean yeah, it's sort of cute, it's just...a bit much.

The timer I'd set on my phone a few minutes ago goes off. It's time. The little plastic stick has my results waiting in its tiny window. Results I'm not ready to look at yet. Because if I don't look, it can't be true.

Bile burns the back of my throat, and I reach the toilet just in time to dry heave into the bowl.

Afterward, I drag myself back over to the sink and rinse my mouth out with cool water.

I need to check the stick. Just get it over with. If I let it sit too long, the results will be inaccurate.

There's a knock on the door.

"Frankie, are you okay in there?"

My mother's voice makes my heart lurch. I quietly scramble to put a hand against the door so she can't come in.

"I'm fine. Be out in a minute."

"You work soon. You're going to be late."

"I know, Mom. I'm just...getting ready to leave."

"All right. Well, I'm going out now. See you tonight, darling."

She makes it sound like we're going to have a cozy dinner for two and then watch a movie together while she braids my hair and asks me about boys. You know, the things I wish she'd done when it still counted.

I don't respond, just listen for her footsteps to fade away. She's right. I am going to be late for work. And I can't avoid this knowledge forever.

Screwing up my courage, I step back over to the bathtub, reach for the stick, and grip it in my fingers. This is it.

Am I about to become a single mother? Will Dante come for the child? Just how badly would he want his baby, his heir? I don't doubt he'd fight me in court for custody. A chill goes through me. He's played me so much. How can I trust that he'll do what's right for this child?

On the other hand, if it's negative, I'm free to move on. To pocket some cash from the crappy waitressing gig until I have enough saved to get my own place, find a better job that will help support Livvie until she's graduated from college. The sky really will be the limit. Because the last thing I want is to be trapped again. I can't handle any more lies or betrayal.

Either way, I know I'll have my hands full regardless of what the results are. There is no life for Dante and me, but being a single mother isn't ever what I had in mind for myself. I'd always hoped that if I did have kids, I'd have more to offer them than the kind of unpredictable, unstable life I'd grown up with. And yet here we are.

Letting out a slow breath, I open my eyes and look at the stick.

Two blue lines.

Holy. Shit.

I'm pregnant. With Dante's child.

My face flames hot as nausea roils in my belly again, the bathroom suddenly seeming smaller and hotter somehow. Sweat beads my hairline and beneath my arms, a hot tingle going down my spine. I can't believe it. I'm pregnant.

And I'm definitely going to throw up again.

2

FRANKIE

"Okay, so that's two patty melts, one with fries, one with a salad, burger of the day, and an order of chicken strips with fries," I say as I set down each plate at table ten. "All good?"

The family of four are all staring at me as if I just served them dog food.

"Where's my mozzarella sticks?" the oldest kid whines, crossing his arms.

"I wanted curly fries!" his little sister says with a pout.

"This has cheese on it. I'm lactose intolerant." The mother shoves her plate toward the end of the table, nearly tipping it onto the floor.

I'm close to reminding her that by default, a patty melt contains cheese, hence the whole "melt" part, which is clearly stated on the menu. But like a good little waitress, I keep my mouth shut. This is my third table today where I haven't gotten a single order right, somehow. It seems like I can't concentrate on anything thanks to those two blue lines.

I force a smile and pick up the plates with the wrong orders.

"So sorry about that, everyone. I'll get this fixed up right away, find the missing mozzarella sticks, and how about some free milkshakes for the inconvenience?"

The dad tilts his head as if he's trying to decide if that's good enough compensation, and then he smiles. "Why not? Thank you."

"No problem." I hesitate a moment, expecting the supposedly "dairy sensitive" mother to remind me again about her lactose intolerance, but she says nothing. Right.

I take the patty melt and the chicken strips back into the kitchen and make an apologetic face at Ruben, the short order cook. He's usually all smiles, but now he frowns. "What happened?"

"The mom at table four is lactose intolerant. Apparently, she's also illiterate. The chicken strips need curly fries instead, and..." I trail off as I double-check the order written in my notepad—and confirm that the kid did not, in fact, ask for mozzarella sticks. "I was told an order of moz sticks is missing." I look up. "Which isn't actually true."

He grins with a little chuckle and takes the plates. "I'll fry up some cheese and make her a meltless patty, then. How 'bout I box this one up and set it in the break room fridge for you?"

"You're willing to risk Charles's wrath? You know how pissed he gets when employees take food." Even as I warn the cook, I'm secretly thanking Ruben profusely in my mind. I'm not sure how I can throw up fifteen times every morning, and then be ravenously hungry by 11 a.m.

Not that it matters. Whatever I eat inevitably comes back up anyway. It's a never-ending cycle.

"Oh heck, what Charles doesn't know won't hurt him," Ruben says, already sliding the chicken strips with the corrected curly fries back toward me as a cheeseless beef patty sizzles on the griddle behind him.

I smile apologetically. "Also, um, I promised them free shakes if they didn't have a fit. I can't really afford any more complaints to the manager this week."

Ruben just nods as he keeps an eye on his work. Hiding a hamburger from our manager is one thing, but fudging four milkshakes is another story. I'll have to be sneaky and quick.

It'll only take a few more minutes for him to finish the patty no-melt and get a fresh batch of cheese sticks cooked up in the fryer, so I grab the milk and ice cream and rush to get the milkshake machine going.

As it whirs, Ruben says, "You had anything to eat today, girly?"

Glancing over, I catch him giving me a caring side-eye. I haven't told anyone about my pregnancy, but judging by the amount of care that the older Cuban man has been giving me since I started working here, I get the feeling that he knew before I did.

"I'm fine," I tell him, removing the metal cups and pouring the shakes into glasses.

I'm putting the glasses on my tray when Charles saunters over. Which, of course he does. My boss is almost always watching me.

"What's this?" he asks.

His belly hangs well over his belt, and I quietly hope that he doesn't get too close to me and knock my tray out of my hands. It wouldn't be the first time his girth has gotten in the way. His downturned mustache matches his perpetual frown. He's just an unpleasant person, all around. But this diner pays higher than anywhere else in town, so for now I'm trying to keep him happy.

"Shakes for table four," I say casually, trying to sneak around him.

He waves a small stack of tickets in his hand. "There are no milkshakes on any of your orders. Why did you make them?"

Classic Charles. I swear the man gets some kind of thrill out of double-checking every ticket against every food item that goes out of the kitchen.

There's no use trying to lie to him, so I try to just smile my way through it. "It's all good, Charles. My treat for the family. I'll pay for them with tips before the end of my shift."

"Your *treat*?" His expression says he's not buying it. In fact, I'm sure he knows exactly what happened—he just can't pass up a chance to berate and humiliate me. "Had another screwup, Frankie?"

It's obvious he's getting some perverse joy out of this. His voice is loud enough to be clearly heard over the noise in the kitchen, and I'm sure the customers sitting out at the counter can hear every word.

"Something like that," I say, my fake smile starting to strain my cheeks.

"I don't know why I don't just fire you," he goes on. "You're definitely not the hard worker you said you'd be when I interviewed you."

There's so much I'd like to say in response, but I bite my tongue. He walks away and I finish loading my tray, swearing to myself that I'll start looking for a new job tomorrow. One that will let me go on maternity leave after a few months on the payroll. Nothing is worth getting treated like this.

But until then, I'm stuck here. I have to save enough money to get my own place. My mother and I circle each other like prickly hedgehogs, and Miggy won't stop eating my shoes. If only I could sell the Jaguar...but I don't have the title. I guess I could sell it to someone shady online, but I'm too worried about getting ripped off or robbed at the handoff—or worse. Not only that, but I have to admit that the few sweet minutes of freedom I get cruising to and from work with the top down are basically the only bright spots in my life right now.

Ruben rings the bell, indicating my corrected orders are ready.

"Thanks, Ruben," I say. "You're too good to me."

"Don't mention it. And don't worry about the boss. This place is just a pitstop for you. You got better things ahead."

"Thanks." If only I could believe that.

I just need to keep on scouring the Internet and the local papers for a better opportunity. Unfortunately, there isn't much need for a sommelier around here. It's not like I can just walk into a winery and get a job. The market here is nothing compared to what it is in Napa. At best, I might be able to work in the alcohol department of a grocery store.

Not that it would pay nearly what I'd need to get an apartment on my own—even a crappy studio runs just under a thousand dollars a month, and minimum wage here is only ten an hour. There's no way in hell I'm raising my baby in a shabby place, either. I need money. I need a better job. Dammit, I just need a break.

I deliver the corrected meals and the milkshakes to table four, check on my other customers, warm up a few coffees, and settle a few tabs. As I drop off receipts and change, a wave of dizziness goes through me. Putting my hand on the counter to steady myself, I take a few deep, slow breaths. I really need to eat. Carla, one of the other waitresses, gives me a curious look.

"You okay, Frankie?"

I nod, glancing around at my tables. My customers are mostly taken care of. "You mind if I take a few minutes in the break room? My tables are set for now."

She shrugs like it's no skin off her back. Nothing phases her, ever.

The ties of my apron suddenly feel too tight, so I loosen them as I make my way back to the break room. True to his word, Ruben hid my burger in the fridge. I don't even bother to heat it up as I sink down in a folding chair and wolf it down.

The first bite is incredibly delicious, but it's hard not to dream about Alain's food. God, how I miss his cooking. I like to think I never took having a personal chef for granted, but considering that neither my mother nor I can cook—and we can't afford takeout every night—I'd do literally anything for one of Alain's meals right now. I've been living off of diner leftovers and scrambled eggs and ramen noodles, but I know I have to do better for my baby's sake.

Before I know it, the burger is almost gone. My eyes dart around the break room to see if there's anything else laying out that I can eat. Sometimes Carla brings in those massive, family size multipacks of trail mix, cheese- or peanut butter-filled sandwich crackers, or dried fruit from the big-box store, and she's always generous with them.

But then my stomach gives a familiar roll of nausea. I close my eyes and cross my hands over my stomach. "At least let me finish eating before you squeeze it back out again, baby."

Oh. God. I just spoke to my unborn child. This is really happening.

My hands smooth over my abdomen. I can't feel any changes there yet, but there's a baby inside. A small creation that's part Dante and part me. Mere *months* from now, I'll be holding him or her. It's unbelievable.

I always thought I'd have children someday, but not this soon. I guess with the way my sisters and I grew up, I was afraid of what kind of life I'd be bringing them into. My mom's apartment in Miami isn't exactly worst-case scenario, but it almost feels like it sometimes.

Still, her place is better than being in the clutches of a lying, selfish, greedy-ass manipulative bastard of a husband.

Tearing into the last few bites of my burger, I try to push away all thoughts of Dante and focus on getting this food down. Afterward I wipe my mouth, take a long drink of water, and then pause. For a few seconds, I feel great. And then my stomach lurches.

Bolting out of the chair, I make a run for the dingy employee restroom, where I immediately throw that delicious burger right back up.

Damn.

Well, maybe Ruben will burn something he can set aside for me later.

3

DANTE

Marco and I have been trying to figure out the identity of the man Bregman implicated in our father's murder, but we keep coming up empty-handed.

He sent Bregman's phone to a woman named Yael who we contract with (under the table) for help with tech stuff, but despite her detailed sweep of the cell, it was no dice. The burner phone didn't have any clues as to who—or where—the blonde man might be. To boot, the international number he'd texted from was, in fact, another burner phone. Which meant it wasn't registered to anybody. Yael traced the number to an old school phone card company, but they sell prepaid phones all over the world, so we essentially hit a dead end.

Yael also turned off the tracking on Bregman's phone so that no one would be able to trace it back to us—and so, out of options, we made a last-ditch attempt to pose as Bregman and text the blonde man. But our efforts to fool him into dropping clues hadn't worked. After our initial exchanges, we didn't receive any more responses. Marco says there was probably some kind of code word in the texts that we didn't reply to properly.

We do, however, continue to receive texts from Bregman's employer, girlfriend, and mother. Concerned at first that he's missing, then angry that he apparently skipped town, and finally back to more concern and even panic. My insides go sour every time another message comes through. One of them will be calling the cops any day now, and we'll have to destroy the phone for good.

This whole business with Bregman has been one more reminder of why my brothers and I are divesting ourselves for good of the sordid empire our father built.

Still, knowing that people care about Bregman doesn't make me regret putting him out of his misery for the part he played in my father's murder—and would have played in Marco's, if he'd gotten the chance to tamper with Marco's race car. Hell, I'd kill a hundred Bregmans to keep my family safe.

Even with Bregman out of the way, I can't stop thinking about somebody tampering with my little brother's car. Marco is reckless in almost every aspect of his life. Speed and adrenaline feed him. And while I'm sure his team is careful to check over his vehicle before he gets on the track, a skilled professional mechanic would know how to subtly tamper with it. I've had dreams almost every night of Marco's Porsche going up in a ball of flame.

And if Marco is a target, I'm sure that Armani and myself are too. Likely Frankie as well. I don't know yet how deep this goes, but we're going to find out.

Speaking of Frankie, my wife has been gone for several weeks now. My calls and texts to her initially went unanswered, and then were blocked. So I went back and retraced her activities the last day I saw her, which led me to Ruby. She'd told me all about the financial documents Frankie had demanded for review. Including one very incriminating one.

"If you need to fire me, Mr. Bellanti, I understand," Ruby had said, chin up.

"Ruby, you've been working in these offices for almost forty years," I told her. "You're not going anywhere. Unless you want to."

She'd shaken her head emphatically. "I care about my job, and I care about your family. I'd like to stay."

That loyalty is exactly why I'd never fire Ruby.

On top of which, she's a damn good admin. Competent, professional, highly discreet when necessary, and generally very pleasant.

What's not so pleasant is the fact that my wife knows everything now. About the debts I forgave... and the one I didn't. Her own family's debt.

And while she has no idea why I did the things the way that I did, knowing her, she assumed the worst. And then she ran. Even though she had everything she could have possibly wanted here.

Well. Maybe not everything. I never gave her the full truth.

Obviously I know exactly where she is and what she's been doing since she left. I'd turned on the GPS theft tracker on the Jag soon after she turned up missing, and watched her drive clear across the country. Straight to her mother's place in Miami. Which I admit did surprise me. I would have checked a very long list of places before even considering looking for Miriam Abbott, who also goes by Miriam Wright, and who works a part-time job at some women's boutique in Coral Gables and appears to have an active social life. Armani hasn't had any trouble digging up information.

It's taken all my willpower not to force Frankie to come home. In truth, the only reason I haven't tried is because I don't know if it would work. And if she runs again, she won't be so sloppy with the trail of breadcrumbs next time. She's a clever woman, even if she gets some of her facts muddled from time to time. At least with her in Miami, I can keep tabs on her.

I get up from my desk and take my tablet over to the window to look once more at the photos Armani's surveillance guy sent me this morning. Good God, Frankie is really bad at waitressing.

The Miami-based associate Armani hired has been following her around for weeks, sending images to Armani's phone a few times a day. I've seen pictures of her spilling a drink on a customer's lap, dropping a plate of fries on the floor, getting yelled at by her boss—which pisses me off. I make a mental note to find out his name as I swipe to another image of Frankie, wearing the best resting-bitch face I've ever seen as a customer appears to be complaining.

Enough is enough. What is she getting out of all this?

How can this be what she really wants?

Frankie belongs here, at Bellanti Vineyards. She belongs with *me*. As the weeks have gone by, my patience has worn thin. What was slightly amusing at first is now a constant source of frustration and ill temper. I've mostly taken it out on Armani.

As if on cue, I hear a rap on my office door and look up to see him letting himself in.

"I don't believe I invited you in," I tell him coldly.

My brother just ignores me, pointing to the photo on the screen.

"I sent that guy in there to act like a customer and leave her a big tip," he says. "A very generous one."

Slamming the tablet down, I spear him with a glare. "Why the hell would you do that? I want this to be hard on her, not let her skate through. She needs to fail so she can decide to come home. Do you think she'll do that if people are tipping her generously?"

"Calm down. I felt bad for her. Not that it made a difference."

He picks up the tablet and scrolls to the next image. A busboy is looking over his shoulder as he slips the three one-hundred dollar bills off the table and into his apron pocket.

"Okay, good. She needs to hit rock bottom."

Armani doesn't hide his annoyance. "Says the man who made her run off in the first place."

"That's assumptive of you," I snap. I haven't discussed the reasons behind Frankie's disappearance with him, and he never asked.

"Would there be another reason for her to take off *besides* you?"

Fuck. I want to be angry with my brother, but he's right. I am the reason she's gone.

"I may not have been completely honest with her about...a few things," I admit.

"Wow. Imagine that. You, not being honest."

I shoot him a glare. "Are you trying to piss me off?"

My brother just shrugs. Deep restlessness courses through me and I look back out the window, seeing nothing but the green blur of the grounds.

"Look, Dante. In a way, I don't blame her. You should have just told her the truth."

That's real fucking helpful. "Stay out of it," I growl.

"Is this really what you want for your wife? Or would you consider actually talking to her and sorting this out?"

"When you get your own wife, you can do things your way," I tell him. "Until then, you can fuck off."

He doesn't answer. I spin in time to see him opening the door and letting himself out.

A frustrated growl loosens from my throat as I return to the window and press a fist against the glass. Francesca is good at wine. Very good. She's one of the most knowledgeable and skilled professionals I've ever met, and I know a lot of people in the industry. She was made to do this. Not waitress at some shithole. Not spend her days living in a subpar neighborhood.

Anything could happen to her there. Bad people, a drug bust gone wrong. Drive-by shootings. My mind races with every possible disaster.

I don't want her living that life any longer. So she's not going to.

She *is* my wife. And dammit, I'm going to get her.

4

FRANKIE

I spy the stream of dog drool and move out of the way before it lands on me.

"No, Miggy! Go away!" I shoo him with a wave of my arm, but the meathead just sits down and stares at me, long strings of drool hanging from his droopy jowls. I just got home, and barely had time to collapse onto the couch before he trotted right over to spatter me with his slime.

"Francesca, don't yell at him! He's a helpless dog."

My mother's voice streams from the kitchen. It smells like she's making mac and cheese, the one thing we can both whip up without burning.

"I just want to lie down for a few minutes without this furball bothering me," I shout back through the doorway. "It's not too much to ask."

"He's a *dog*. He's happy to see you. It's his nature."

I flop an arm over my eyes and kick my feet up onto the cushions. "Well, I'm not happy to see him."

My entire body aches. My guts are still on fire from multiple rounds of tossing my cookies, and I've had a tension headache pulsing behind my eyes since noon. I'm pretty sure I paid out more than I made today covering all the free milkshakes I'd had to give to customers to make up for getting their orders wrong. I had one happy patron, but for some reason he didn't tip me.

A hot wave of dog breath washes over my face, and I open my eyes and glare at the dog.

"Miggy, go see Mommy in the kitchen, okay? Go get some mac and cheese." He doesn't budge. Naturally. "C'mon, Miggy. Go! Get!"

My mother appears around the corner, stirring a pot with a wooden spoon. "Oh, Francesca, just pet him a little and he'll leave you alone."

Oh, hell no. That's *it*.

"Don't CALL ME THAT!" I shout, loud enough to be heard over the dog's incessant panting.

My mom freezes, looking almost shocked at my outburst. Since my arrival, she's appeared unflappable. Now, her eyes narrow and her mouth turns down as if I've offended her.

"It's your name," she replies softly. "I gave it to you. I didn't give you much in this world, I know that, but I did name all of my girls. And I named them well, Francesca Carina Abriana Abbott."

Sitting up on the couch, I bury my face in my hands. My eyes burn and I can't hold back tears. Everything is rushing at me all at once, and at the center of it all is Dante.

There's a metallic clunk as my mother sets the pot on the coffee table. Her gentle weight sinks into the couch cushion next to me, her hand warm where she presses it against my back. I want to fight her attempt at motherly interest, but I don't have it in me.

"Frankie. What's wrong?"

"*He* called me Francesca," I choke out between sniffles. "And I'm so tired of thinking about him."

There's a beat of silence and then my mom starts rubbing small circles over my back.

"Dante?" she says, so quietly it's almost a whisper.

"I don't want to talk about him. I—I can't." My voice cracks on the last word.

"You don't have to," she says. "I'm not trying to pry. But I want you to know...well...you certainly wouldn't be the first woman in history to choose the wrong man. Myself included, God knows. But that doesn't mean you have to suffer for it. There's absolutely no shame in leaving him, darling. Do what's best for you. I support you, no matter what you choose."

As if it's that easy.

I swipe tears from my eyes and shake my head. "That's just it, Mom. I didn't *choose* him. Dad arranged the marriage, to repay a debt. I had no choice but to go through with it."

Just like that, the whole tumultuous story is spilling out. My mom doesn't say anything as I ramble on about my disastrous marriage, the ups and downs, how I went from despising Dante to loving him without even realizing it. And how easily he can tear me down. There's a soft weight on my leg. Miggy is resting his head on my knee. I didn't even realize he'd come closer.

I pat his head absently as I finish with, "Even if I can get through divorcing him, I'll still be stuck with him forever."

My mom's brows draw together. "Why do you say that?"

No point in holding back. "I'm pregnant."

"Oh, Frankie." She takes my hands in hers and runs her thumbs over my knuckles.

Another wave of tears hits me, and she gets up and returns with a box of tissues. I grab a handful to blot my eyes and my mom sits down next to me again.

"This all must be terrifying for you. But you're not alone, sweetie. Even though I couldn't be there for you while you were growing up, I will *always* be here for you and this baby now."

I nod as I stroke the dog's fur, so emotionally raw that I can't form a proper response.

"And I'm sorry about your marriage, Frankie. I never thought your father would do something like this to you."

A flash of anger hits me, and I huff a sarcastic laugh. "How could you? You had no idea what was going on at home after you walked out."

"I know. I let you and your sisters down, and I am sorry. But it wasn't like you think."

"How was it, then?" I ask, no malice in my voice—just curiosity. I've always wanted answers about why she left, and today might be the day I finally get them.

"He blackmailed me, Frankie. I didn't want to leave, but...I had no choice. He forced me to abandon you. That's the truth."

Her voice is thick with unshed tears. Our eyes connect. I've never seen her so quietly desperate. She takes a shaky breath, and my body goes tight with anticipation...and foreboding.

"I wanted to divorce your father after his gambling had gotten out of control the first time. We were on the verge of losing everything. Strange men were knocking on our door at all hours of the night, demanding to see him. He'd come home with split lips, black eyes, an empty bank account. And the drinking...I went weeks without seeing him sober. And he was so mean.

"So one day I stayed up late and waited for him to come home, and told him I was going to file for divorce and take the three of you with me when I left. I said he could clean up his act and get a lawyer if he wanted to try for shared custody—"

"Did you actually think he'd do that?" I ask.

"I wanted to give him a chance, and I really hoped he would. Hoped he cared enough about his daughters to get sober and quit gambling. But until then, I said, I wouldn't let him be a part of our lives. Of course, he was furious. He went ballistic. Breaking things, yelling, how dare I take his family away, that kind of thing. But then he calmed down. He talked to me—admitted he had a problem, promised he'd get help. He *wanted* to get help. Get better, for all of us."

I nod as she talks, her description of my father's manipulations exactly on point.

"But his debts...that was something he couldn't fix by himself. But he said I could."

This is definitely a twist I didn't see coming. "Wait, you? How?"

My mother straightens her shoulders as if she's gathering courage.

"It turned out that one of your father's... associates...had made it obvious that he was interested in me. So your dad made an indecent proposal. I would spend one night in this man's bed, and in return, he would cover your father's debts."

"*What?*" My stomach drops. I can't believe what I'm hearing.

"I know. And at first, I said there was no way I would even consider it. But your father convinced me it was the only way. He needed a clean slate to get on the road to recovery. So I...eventually agreed. I wanted him to get better, for you and your sisters, even though I wasn't going to stay with him. I did have love for him. He was the father of my children, after all."

I still can't wrap my head around this. "But Mom—"

"Of course, it was all a lie." She lets out a bitter laugh. "Your father got his money, but my 'activities' were photographed, video recorded to make me look like an adulterer. I wouldn't get a cent in court if I filed for a divorce, and I'd be painted as a whore, an unfit mother."

Everything she's saying has the unmistakable ring of truth—an ugly truth. I'm in shock.

"Your father promised he'd take care of you, give you every opportunity, make it so you three would live like royalty in that big house with the horses and all the land. But I had to walk away, or else he'd divorce me and leave me with nothing, make sure you kids had nothing, too. I never thought, never in a million years, that he wouldn't keep his word."

Live like royalty? Yeah—in the sense that my sisters and I grew up unloved, kept in the background, more or less raised by a succession of housekeepers... and that I'm now in an arranged marriage. I'd say my father definitely accomplished the whole royalty thing.

"It's not your fault, Mom," I tell her. "And I'm—I'm sorry he did that to you."

"No, don't apologize for him. I'm the one who's sorry. But we did have happy times, Frankie. He *loved* you girls. I truly thought I was doing what was best. I swear, if I'd suspected what he was capable of, how it would all play out, I would've never left."

Both of us are crying now, passing the tissue box back and forth. Miggy is panting at our feet, clearly distressed at seeing us like this. When my mom finally calms down a bit, she fixes a regretful gaze on me.

"Has Dante...ever asked you to do something like I had to do?" she asks carefully. "Something you weren't comfortable with, or...pushed you too hard in bed?"

I don't always trust Dante to do the right thing—if I did, I wouldn't be here right now. But I can't imagine him ever doing something like what my father did to my mom.

"No," I say firmly. "Things between us, in that way, have always been...consensual. Maybe not loving, at least not in the beginning. But toward the end, there was love. I'm sure of it."

"I'm so glad."

My mother wraps me in a tight hug. I hesitate for a moment before lightly hugging her back. I can't remember the last time she spoke to me like this. Or held me.

"But I still wish I could punch Dante right in the nose for you," she goes on.

That gets a weak laugh out of me. "Me, too."

"I know I wasn't around to say it, but I do love you. And your sisters." She squeezes me tighter. This time, I lean into it.

"I think on some level, I knew you did. That was what made you leaving so much worse."

She just holds me close, as if she can put me back together through sheer force of will.

And maybe herself, too.

5

FRANKIE

Someone is breathing heavily in my ear.

I sit upright, heart racing at the unexpected sound, when I realize it's just Miggy with his head resting on the side of the bed, staring at me.

"Go away, dog breath," I tell him.

He, of course, doesn't listen—just gives me eyes of love. And all right, fine, he *is* freaking adorable. Still doesn't mean I want him waking me up with his foul panting in my face.

Groggy, I flop back down onto the pillows. Miggy. I turn my head and stare into the dog's brown eyes. Miggy...where have I heard that before? Charlie, Frankie, Livvie...Miggy.

Huh.

The more I try to catch the thread, the faster it slips away, and then whatever thought I'm trying to form quickly disappears as the first wave of morning sickness hits me.

I squeeze my eyes shut, trying to will the nausea away. I'm underslept, mentally drained, and not a single part of me aside from my stomach wants to get up right now, even though my alarm is going to go off soon anyway. My mother's confession kept playing in my head long after I'd gone to bed last night, and it took me forever to fall asleep as I skated through an obstacle course of emotions, most of them heated and pointed in my father's direction.

Bile rises in my throat, and I have no choice but to leap off the bed. I nearly stumble over the dog, who runs after me as I hurry into the hall. A familiar clench bands beneath my ribs and I barely make it to the bathroom before my first puke of the day.

Yay. Just how I like to start my morning.

I hear my cell phone alarm go off in my bedroom and I groan. Time to get ready for work—the last thing I want to do today.

I manage to wash my face, brush my teeth, and throw my hair into a ponytail while expending as little energy as possible. It's going to take all my willpower to get through my shift. Lack of sleep and the mental load of my father's nastiness are not mixing well with my pregnancy hormones.

There's a note from my mother on the kitchen

table along with an odd-looking fruit that resembles a small, light orange tomato.

Persimmons helped me when I was pregnant with you girls. Careful though, Miggy likes—

Before I can finish reading, the dog snatches the persimmon from my fingers and chomps it in half, quickly wolfing it down in two bites. Stupid dog. But he looks so damned pleased with himself that I can't help laughing at him.

Oh well. Might as well barf up a banana as a persimmon.

Along with the banana, I bag up a sleeve of saltine crackers and a bottle of water for my drive to work. Breakfast of champions. Then I put Miggy in his crate and quickly slip into my polyester waitress outfit and clunky white tennis shoes.

I swear, I'll never get used to the heat here. Within minutes, the uniform is sticking to my skin. My feet sweat and the hairline at the base of my neck is getting damp. Despite the air conditioning in the apartment, I constantly feel like I'm sweltering. I don't know how anybody chooses to live here long term. Then again, I've probably been spoiled by Northern California.

I feel a pang of homesickness for Napa, but I squash it.

There's some commotion outside the building as

I exit the apartment. My mom's neighbor Teresa and her teenage son are putting up Christmas decorations around their patio—right alongside the Thanksgiving decor. Glittery tinsel hangs next to pumpkins and striped gourds, plastic turkeys in pilgrim hats, and bunches of colorful corn. The teenager is currently up on a ladder, hanging glass ornaments from the roof overhang. Teresa waves cheerily.

"Frankie, good morning."

"Good morning," I answer back.

Both of them are dressed in tank tops, shorts, and flip-flops. Kinda boggles the mind. It never got much below 40° in Napa (if it did, it never would have become wine country), but at least it cooled down enough to enjoy the changing of the seasons. Here? Not so much. I'm sure it's sweltering year-round.

"It's so nice of you to stay with your mother for a while," Teresa is saying. "You know, she's always been a lovely neighbor. And Miggy is such a gentle giant."

"Yes, he is. And that's nice to hear."

My outfit is beginning to itch. I need to get in my car and crank the air conditioning, stat.

"We just love the Christmas season," she goes on. "We couldn't wait to put these out. You and your mom should decorate your porch this year! Let us know if we can help."

I have no idea if my mother decorates for the holidays or not, but I force a smile.

"Oh, yeah. I'll mention it to her. That's a good idea." I'm not trying to be rude, but I feel like I'm melting, and the heat isn't making my nausea any better. "Anyway, I better get going. Don't want to be late for my shift!"

I give a little wave and hurry to my car before she can start talking again.

The air conditioning inside the car feels so good that I take the long way to the diner. I feel slightly better by the time I arrive, until I find Charles waiting for me in the back. I hang up my purse and clock in, ignoring his glare and his trademark frown.

As I tie my apron on, I start babbling in self-defense. "Before you say anything, Charles, I promise that I'm going to do better today. I know I've been a little off my game lately, but it's just a stomach bug I've had that's been throwing me. I just need another chance."

He puts his hands on his hips. "Another chance for what? To see if you can break your milkshake record?"

Without waiting for my response, he walks away.

Sighing, I grab an order pad and a few pens and shove them into my apron pocket as I walk through the kitchen toward the front of the house. I can see the dining room from here. It's already packed, of course.

Something pulls my attention and I do a double take. I know the glossy head of dark hair in booth seven. The set to the shoulders, the expression carved from stone. But the face doesn't even register with me for a few seconds. And then I push my way through the swinging double doors, and the man in the booth turns his head my way. That's when it fully hits me.

It's Dante.

My breath catches in my throat, and I spin right around and walk back into the kitchen. Fuck. He's real. Fuuuuuck.

"You okay, Frankie?" Ruben asks from his usual post at the griddle.

"I'm good," I lie, giving him a weak smile as my stomach churns.

What the hell is Dante doing here? It's been over three weeks and he's made no attempt to contact me. I had hoped that meant he was letting me go. But now, out of the blue, he's here. And of course, he's sitting at one of my tables.

Does he know about the baby somehow?

Double fuck.

I could try putting him off on another waitress, but he's already seen me. I have no choice but to go over there. Pulling a deep breath through my nose, I go back out to the dining room, walk straight to Dante's booth, and flip open my order pad. I avoid his eyes, keeping my distance.

"What can I get you?" I ask stiffly.

"What do you recommend?" Oh, fuck him. Sitting here trying to be cute.

"For you? Anything I can scrape off the top of the garbage."

"Hm. How's the coffee here?"

I don't write anything down, just glare at him. "It's coffee."

A hint of a smile crosses his lips. "You're a terrible waitress."

"And you're a shit husband," I hiss. "You want fries with that?"

His voice drops intimately. "I want you to come home."

The din of chatting customers, silverware scraping on plates, and clunking water glasses is loud in my ears, but I'm hyper focused on what he's going to say next. What the hell did he come three thousand miles from home to say to me?

"You're my wife," he says. "You have a duty to me, and to the winery."

Really? That's the best he can do? He's not even fighting for me, he's ordering me to fall in line. He hasn't apologized, either, or even asked why I left in the first place.

"If you're not going to order anything, you'll have to excuse me. I have work to do."

He glares at me. "Stop wasting everyone's time. You need to come back."

I could not be less impressed with his little speech.

Slipping my order pad into my pocket, I say sweetly, "I'm sorry, but we don't sell doormats here. Maybe you should try the hardware store down the..." My voice trails off as I'm gripped by a familiar wave of nausea. I consider running.

Dante grabs my wrist. "Frankie? Are you okay?"

Bad, bad timing. I try to pull back, but he won't let me go. My insides lurch. There's nothing I can do.

Bending over, I puke in Dante's lap.

6

FRANKIE

Dante leans back in the booth with his arms spread as I heave on his Italian merino trousers.

A collective gasp and disgusted groan go through the diner.

Dante looks shocked. His suit is obviously ruined. So is the appetite of everyone in the restaurant.

"Free milkshakes for everyone!" I say flippantly as I grab a napkin from the table and wipe my mouth.

The couple in the booth next to Dante's gets up and leaves without ordering, and a few more customers waiting up front to be seated decide to walk out instead.

I should care, but I don't.

"Sorry about your suit," I tell Dante, my voice deadpan.

"God, Frankie, are you okay?"

The honest concern in his voice pulls something in my heart, but I don't get a chance to respond as Charles storms over, clipboard clenched in one meaty fist.

"Frankie! What did you *do*?"

Before I can explain, my boss launches into one of his tirades.

"This is unacceptable. First you screw up more orders than I can count, then you practically run the milkshake machine dry, and now you're getting sick on customers. Do you think I—"

"Is this really how you run a business? By forcing an obviously sick woman to work?" Dante says as he gently moves me aside and stands, tall and imposing despite the vomit on his Tom Ford suit. His face is that hard slab of stone I hate so much, but it's not pointed at me this time.

Charles draws back as Dante comes face-to-face with him.

"You should be ashamed of yourself," Dante goes on. "And how do you know she's not infectious?"

The entire restaurant is openly staring at us now.

"Sir, please, keep your voice down," Charles shushes Dante, glancing around nervously.

"Did she fail to mention that she was feeling

unwell?" Dante prods, making no effort to lower his volume.

Charles hesitates. "Not exactly. She said—"

"Ah. Yet you didn't think to assess the severity of her illness in order to determine if she was fit for work."

"I'm hardly qualified to—"

Dante doesn't let my boss get a word in edgewise. "Which she *clearly* is not. Which means you could have easily diverted this disaster by properly doing *your* damn job."

"Sir, please," Charles pleads, sweat visible at his brow.

"It's really not so bad," I cut in. "It's just a banana." I turn back to Dante and say, "I'm sure I can get it cleaned up if you'll just come into the bathroom for a moment. Sir."

Charles hurriedly agrees and herds us toward the back, yelling at a busboy to come clean up the booth. My husband doesn't say another word as I lead him into the men's restroom and lock the door behind us. I can't help feeling a little pleased to note that he's looking green around the gills himself as he swallows hard and loosens his tie.

"Are you going to throw up, too?"

He doesn't respond.

I nudge him with my elbow. "Oh boy. You really are, aren't you?"

"I have a change of clothes in my car. Go get them."

I wait for him to say please, but of course he doesn't.

"Fine," I say. "I could use some air anyway."

I leave him there and take the back door into the alley and then make my way to the street, where there's a line of tourist shops. I don't bother going to his car, nor do I know which one is his anyway. He never said, and I didn't ask. Instead, I pop into a nearby tourist trap and grab him a pair of red, white, and blue swim trunks with glittery stars all over the ass. And a bright orange T-shirt that says, "FBI: Female Body Inspector."

Giggling to myself as I pay with the tip money in my apron, I go back to the diner and knock on the restroom door. When Dante lets me in, I find him in nothing but his briefs, holding on to his keys and his wallet. His suit is stuffed in the trash, and he's looking considerably less green.

I do a double take at his hard body, the smooth olive skin and tight abs bared for my view. For half a heartbeat, I'm so turned on that I stop breathing.

Pregnancy is clearly doing some things to my

hormones, and the urge to jump his bones in this dingy little bathroom is nearly overwhelming.

I thrust the bag at him. "Here. It's the best I could do."

He pulls the clothes out of the bag. His cheeks turn red with anger.

"Your car was locked," I say with a shrug.

"I am *not* wearing this."

"Then don't. Walk out naked for all I care. Maybe one day you'll learn to say *please*."

With that, I glide out of the men's room and head straight to the break room, silently calculating how many milkshakes are going to come out of my paycheck today—in a concerted effort to push back the wave of horniness still washing over me.

My stomach growls painfully, and I realize I'm hungry again. Damn it all. I press a hand to my abdomen and glance around the break room for something to eat. All I see is an open single-serve package of soup crackers on the table. The crackers look stale and broken, but I dump the whole thing into my mouth anyway.

"Imagine that," comes a voice from the doorway. "Here you are, not working, once again."

Fucking Charles.

"Just got the customer cleaned up," I tell him. "Everything's fine now."

"It's not fine, Frankie. It hasn't been fine since I hired you. If I didn't need the help so bad, you'd have been gone already. You know you're the *only* waitress in my thirty years of managing a restaurant who has actually vomited on a customer."

"*Enough.*"

Dante strides in. He's dressed in the outfit I bought him, clearly on his last nerve. And Charles is about to get it.

"I've had enough of your indifference to the health and safety of your staff," he growls. "I'm going to assume that you have no idea who you're dealing with, or you would've thought twice before speaking to my wife that way."

He looks incredibly imposing, despite his ridiculous outfit. It's just an aura that Dante wears. Charles knows he's in deep shit. His face drops, his skin going pale.

"*Wife?*" Charles sputters.

Dante looks at me. "Get your things. You're done for the day." Then he turns his piercing eyes back to my boss. "I'll be taking care of her now, since you've done such a shit job of it. But don't *for a second* think you can get away with treating the rest of your employees so poorly."

Somehow, he's so stern that Charles immediately starts apologizing—which isn't a reaction I've ever gotten from him. Must be nice to be a man. Fuck, how does Dante manage to still be so commanding in that stupid FBI shirt?

Once I grab my things and we're outside, Dante hustles me into his rental car. I don't get a chance to really figure out how I feel about this sudden turn of events as he races through traffic, speeding as if he's on a mission.

We drive for about twenty minutes, taking the causeway over Biscayne Bay, until 195 dumps us out on West 41st Street in Miami Beach.

I'm so busy admiring the view of the ocean that I don't realize we've arrived at our destination until Dante slows to a stop, pulling into the valet line at the Fontainebleau. Where he has a room, apparently.

I gawk out the window, taking in the luxury hotel. I've been wanting to see the inside of this place since I first arrived in Miami, but never felt like I had the right clothing. You have to be dressed to the nines to even walk through the door, and I didn't bring any designer wear with me when I left Napa.

As we wait for a valet, I tear my eyes from the curved white and glass façade of the building and face him. "We need to talk."

"It can wait until we get up to the room."

I don't bother arguing. I'm too exhausted.

The valet pauses when he gets a look at my

husband's outfit. And then he looks to me as if this is some kind of joke, but of course I'm in my tacky polyester waitress dress. Dante throws money at him as he opens the door and slips out.

"Dante Bellanti. Don't lose my keys," he says, and then comes around to open the passenger door for me, helping me out like I'm an invalid.

I don't fight it. I'm too enamored by the sunlight spilling through the glass-paned awning above us, the perfectly manicured tropical foliage all around, the expensive smell of the hotel's signature scent—Green Bamboo—wafting out the doors on a cool wave of air conditioning. Yas.

Just as I suspected, everyone inside is dressed in designer finery. Even those who are dressed more casually, for the pool or other leisure activities, look like a million dollars. Everyone turns to stare at us, my cheap waitress outfit and Dante's FBI shirt drawing more than a few looks.

When we finally get into the elevator, I can't help but laugh. I'm surprised we didn't get kicked out for breaking the dress code. Dante doesn't seem one bit amused.

I barely get a chance to take in the spacious, luxurious suite as Dante steers me immediately into the bedroom and gently pushes me onto the bed.

"You need to rest," he tells me.

He arranges the pillows and blankets, tucking me in like a child, and then draws the shades over the three-sided garden view window before going into the next room. I hear him ordering room service: tea and soup, steamed basmati rice, a carafe of water, and a ginger ale. Everything is happening so fast, and honestly, this mattress feels so amazing that I really could fall asleep. The sheets smell like fresh, air-dried linen. My eyes close, my body relaxes. I'm on a cloud.

"I can't believe you were working while you're sick. What were you thinking?" Dante says, coming back into the room and setting a glass of water on the night table.

I sit up with a sigh. Well, there goes my peace and quiet.

He takes his tablet from its case and turns it on. "I'm going to look up the best doctors in the city and make an appointment so you can see someone today."

"Dante—"

"Don't. You're going."

I frown. His caring attitude conflicts me. On one hand, it's nice to know that he cares. But on the other, it feels like we're just sliding back into the same old familiar routine of him controlling me and ordering me around.

"Look, Dante. I appreciate what you're doing, but I don't want your help."

He looks up. "I'm not worried about getting sick. I just need you to—"

"I'm not *sick*, Dante. I'm pregnant."

7

FRANKIE

THE STONE-COLD EXPRESSION IS BACK.

"Say something." I want to slap the inscrutable look right off his handsome face.

He squints, looking into the air at absolutely nothing. "We're going to have...a baby."

"That *is* what I just said." I cross my arms over my chest.

He opens his mouth but then pauses again. Probably still processing. "A boy or a girl?"

I can't help rolling my eyes. "Right now, it's a lima bean that makes me vomit."

That seems to wake him up. "Wait. You *have* been to a doctor, right?"

My confidence in his knowledge of pregnancy is nil. Hell, I'm a woman and there's a lot I need to learn. But at least I've got the basics down. "First of all, it's way too early to identify any...genitals. And second, no, I haven't been to a doctor yet. I only just found out."

"Jesus, Frankie."

He springs into action and whips out his phone, tapping rapidly at the screen. I get up to look at what he's doing and see search results for "best baby doctor in Miami."

"That's going to give you a list of pediatricians," I point out. "You need to search OBGYN."

He's not listening to me. He scrolls through the results, frowning when he finds picture after picture of physicians with babies and toddlers.

"It doesn't matter anyway. I'm sending you back to Napa in our plane. I'll have Armani take care of everything."

I put a hand on his shoulder. "Dante, stop."

Ignoring me, he opens up his texting app, then turns on the microphone. "Armani, I need you to file a flight plan for the plane, out of Miami-Opa locka into Napa County Airport."

This is getting out of hand fast. "Please just listen to me—"

"And then I need you to find me the best gynecologist in Napa..."

"Dante!" I put my hand over his phone before he can send the message. "We don't need a lady doctor. Aren't you a female body inspector, after all?"

I pry his phone out of his hands, deleting the message he was about to send to his brother. Dante watches me with narrowed eyes.

"What are you talking about?" he asks.

At least he finally slowed his roll.

I point at his ridiculous shirt and he looks down at it, then rips it off with a curse and throws it on the floor. "This isn't a joke, Frankie."

"Have you forgotten how to laugh at yourself already? That's disappointing."

"This isn't the time to—"

Just then, there's a knock at the door and the call of room service.

Cursing under his breath some more, Dante grabs a robe from the closet and throws it on. While he answers the door, I grab the other robe and go into the lush bathroom to draw a bath.

"Not bad," I say out loud.

There's wall-to-wall marble, a deep soaking tub, and a gorgeous view of the ocean out the window. I also find a selection of luxurious bath products lined up on the vanity. Moments later, the whole room smells of lavender and sea breeze, both refreshing and comforting. I need the comfort. Dante isn't even processing the idea of having a child. He's gone straight into work mode, making plans, trying to plot logistics. Controlling every detail. Which I guess is what he does best, but it's really rubbing me the wrong way.

Stripping off my disgusting uniform, I slip into the mountain of fragrant bubbles and sink into the water up to my chin. This isn't exactly how I had hoped to tell Dante that we were expecting. Then again, I hadn't really figured out how—or if—I was going to tell him at all.

Still, it's both comforting and irritating that he showed up here like this. I'm frustrated that he thinks I'm going to just bend to his will and do whatever he tells me to do...and now that he knows about the baby, he's going to expect me to come home. Regardless of what *I* want to do.

Damn him.

I place a damp washcloth over my eyes and block out the world. This tub feels like a slice of heaven. When I hear the bathroom door open a few minutes later, I don't even bother to move. Until Dante gently shifts my shoulders forward and slides down into the bath behind me. His arms and legs envelop me, my head leaning back against his warm, bare chest.

It's hard to breathe with him so close. It's hard to think straight with his naked body wrapped around me. So I don't say anything. I figure I'll let him talk first.

His fingers lightly tug my hair over my shoulder and he caresses the base of my neck. "Frankie, I'm..." His voice trails off.

"Sorry?" I prompt.

"Not used to thinking about other people sometimes," he finishes.

Internally, I deflate. It's definitely not what I wanted to hear.

But then he continues, "I want to take care of you, Frankie, and our baby. I want to give our child a solid, safe future. Nothing like what you and I grew up with."

As he talks, I can't help thinking of my mom, of how different my childhood was from what Dante is promising. Care, support, protection. Stability. I can feel my eyes stinging with tears, even under the cool weight of the washcloth.

Dante reaches around and slips it from my eyes, dipping it in the water before gently washing the tops of my shoulders. Then he lifts my hair and runs the cloth over my neck, my throat, and beneath my jaw. My hormones have me on edge almost immediately.

The light rub of the fabric over my skin, his careful exploration of my body, and the feel of him wet and naked behind me, every bit of it is electrifying. A low moan escapes my lips. He leans me slightly forward and trails the cloth down the exposed part of my spine, my back and around to my ribs.

It feels so good. I've missed his touch, even if I hate to admit it. All of our problems could easily fade away right now. The lies. The mistruths. The withheld information. In this moment, everything is perfect and I'm right where I'm supposed to be. Measuring my breathing, I rest against him once more, giving him full access to my front.

He softly strokes the cloth over my hard nipples before making light circles around them and over my breasts. The unexpected sensations make me tremble, a hot ache growing between my legs. The cloth works lower, over the sensitive edge of my ribs to my belly button, to my abdomen where he ever so gently lays a hand just above my pubic bone. He stays like this for several breaths, him and me breathing together as he wraps around me, keeping us safe.

Then he ditches the washcloth and slips his hand lower, sliding his fingers between my thighs and tracing along my sensitive lips. The press of his mouth beneath my ear nearly sends me into orbit. I reach behind me to cup his head in my palm.

He lightly grabs my wrist. "Let's get out."

"Okay," I murmur.

Dante gets out and quickly dries off, then grabs a huge, fluffy towel and helps me from the tub. He holds my hand and guides me as if I'm fragile. Maybe I am. I don't resist as he dries me, then wraps the towel around my body before picking me up and carrying me to the bed. It's so easy to slide back into that easy place of loving him, wanting him, needing him. So I don't fight it. Not right now.

I want him too much.

Dante takes his time peeling away the towel, as if he's forgotten what I look like naked and he's unwrapping me slowly to enjoy the surprise. Goosebumps light on my skin. He notices and quickly covers me with the soft white down comforter. I open one end in invitation, and once he climbs on top of me, I cover him too.

We're immersed in our little cocoon as he carefully and thoroughly works my body. His touch is tender and gentle in the way he explores me, his lips reverent as he kisses me. I give in, letting myself go completely, reveling in his hands, his lips, breathless with wanting him inside me. But he takes his time, covering me with kisses, inch by inch, refusing to take a single caress of reciprocation. It's like he's worshipping me as I lie there and take all the pleasure he offers.

When he finally thrusts his hot, hard cock into me, stars shoot behind my eyes. It's been too long. Too damn long. Lost in the feel of him, hungry for him to fill me up, I cry out as the pleasure flames bright, expanding, building, so fast I can't stop it, until I'm tossed over the edge. An orgasm shockwaves through me, quickly followed by another that bypasses the first and floods me harder than any climax ever has. Meanwhile he pushes into me with strained, measured thrusts, as if he's purposely holding himself back.

"It's okay. You're not going to hurt me," I tease.

The words no sooner leave my mouth then he pounds into me, groaning hard, his release spilling inside me with a hot gush that leaves us both gasping for air.

Afterward, Dante gathers me in his arms, a possessive hand on my still-flat belly. Soon enough, the even rise and fall of his chest tells me he's drifted off, but I'm not so lucky. I can't quiet my mind.

The FBI shirt is wadded up on the floor where Dante threw it earlier. I can't hold back a smile. Even if Dante didn't see the humor in it, I did, and I'll never forget the look of horror on his face when he pulled it out of the bag.

He's a much better man than my father—that's not in doubt. With him, I know I'll always have security. Gourmet food, a castle of a house, designer clothes, money. My baby and I will have all the trappings of a steady, stable life.

But I can't help feeling that it is, indeed, a trap.

8

DANTE

For the first time in far too long, I wake up with Francesca in my arms.

Her warm body pressed against me feels like a dream at first, until I skim her bare skin with my palm and weave my fingers into her silky hair. Francesca. She's really here with me.

Francesca. The mother of my child. *Our* child.

I can still scarcely believe it. I'm going to be a father.

It had always been there, of course—the idea that I would have children. My father had drilled it into my brothers and me that upholding and continuing the family line was critical. The fact that I'd eventually become a father was inevitable. But now that it's real...it feels different. Having it actually happening right now feels nothing like merely being aware that it would come to pass at some future point in time.

So here I am, holding the woman who's carrying my child. Is it a son, or a daughter? I look up to the ceiling in the soft morning light. Do I even care? I don't know anything about raising a child. But a son, I can figure out. As for a daughter...I don't really know what I could offer a daughter. The parenting example I'd gotten from my father—the violence, the scheming, the murder and intrigue—that was all over now. A way of doing things that my brothers and I would never carry on.

As for my mother...I barely remember her. I know she was warm, funny, and attentive. But only in a general sense. I struggle to recall actual memories of her. It's like she's faded to a gentle blur over the years, along with my sister. Had they been around while I was growing up, I'm sure I'd be more well-versed in how to interact with females, but as it is, I'm constantly feeling my way in the dark. And it's not like Frankie had it much better, considering that her father is a monster and her mother walked out on them. What the hell kind of parents will we be?

We'll be better together, won't we? We'll get help. They have counselors and books and TED Talks to help people be good parents. I'll do some research, make a list. Find the best parenting books.

And pregnancy books, too. She's going to need birthing classes. No, *we're* going to need birthing classes. And then during the actual labor part...how am I going to get through all the screaming and pushing and bodily fluids?

Oh, God.

I can feel my blood pressure rising, my skin getting uncomfortably hot. Air. I need air.

Gently shifting Frankie off me, I ease toward the edge of the bed and sit up, trying to take slow, calming breaths. Panic is not useful. But planning is. Making plans for the future is a much better use of my time than worrying about things I can't control. I guess that's one thing my father taught me that actually turned out to be useful. Maybe there's hope for me after all.

And even though I can't change the way my father raised me, I *can* be sure that I don't make the same mistakes. It's bad enough I wasn't there for Frankie when she got the results of her pregnancy test—I've already missed one pivotal moment of being a parent. I won't miss anything else.

Slipping off the bed, I quickly dress in slacks and a shirt and head into the suite's separate living room area. I sit on the sofa and pull up the calendar on my phone so I can try to figure out when Frankie likely conceived and when the baby will be born. I do the math in my head and come up with some ballpark dates for conception and delivery. We still have some time to get everything in order. But I know the time is going to go fast, and there's so much to do.

We should start looking for an au pair. Whomever we hire will be living in our house, of course, so she'll have to be carefully vetted. Especially considering that someone is gunning for my family. We can't be too cautious.

My blood nearly freezes at the thought of something happening to my wife and child. Jesus, and what if my family's enemies find out about the pregnancy? It'd put a target right on Frankie's back. She's going to need to be protected at all times. Around the clock.

I stand and begin pacing the room. I'll assign Donovan to her full-time and make sure he's well-armed. Maybe I'll call on a few of the cousins in Chicago—see if there's any way I can get some of them to come stay on the Bellanti property and stand guard detail for the next year or so. Maybe Frankie should have more than one bodyguard…and our kid is certainly going to need one.

We don't know how far the threat to our family extends, who all is against us, or even how safe we'll be once we find and dispose of the person—or people—who ordered my father's death. Right now, anyone even associated with the Bellantis could be at risk. Especially if our enemies don't succeed at breaching the Bellanti compound or taking out my brothers and me. They'll be getting more and more desperate.

Dammit. Bregman's inability to help identify the man targeting us has put my entire extended family in the worst kind of limbo. We know the threat is out there, but we don't have any idea where it's coming from. So we're sitting here twiddling our fucking thumbs, waiting for the enemy to make the next move. But I refuse to let my family be a bunch of sitting ducks.

In fact, Frankie shouldn't even leave the house—but I know that's not realistic. She'll need medical care, and so will the baby. Plus, she'd go stir crazy. I've already put her through enough, and I can't expect her to live like a hermit until the threat has been fully terminated.

That settles it, then. She's getting a full guard detail.

First things first, I'll get my hands on an armored SUV for Donovan to use. We'll have to make a schedule of her comings and goings so I always know where she is, expand the property's security features, and hire more guards. Maybe I should look into guard dogs, too. Trained attack dogs with excellent temperaments, the kind that are safe to have around children.

My mind is racing now. I grab a hotel pen and notepad, open up my laptop, and set myself up on the sofa again, furiously making lists and drafting emails.

I only take a break to make a pot of coffee in the suite's kitchen, and once I have a steaming cup in my hand, I dial Armani. It's still somewhat early on the West Coast, but we need to talk.

The second he answers his phone, I blurt out, "She's pregnant."

Silence fills the line.

"Is this...good news?" he asks carefully.

"Yeah. It is."

Armani lets out a relieved-sounding laugh. "Then congratulations, man. I'm thrilled for you both. This is wild. So what's next? What can I do?"

"First things first, we've got to make some immediate changes in security."

"What exactly do you have in mind?"

Glancing at the list I made earlier, I say, "Let's get into contact with the cousins in Chicago. We need armed men."

"Sure. What else?"

"Extra security around the winery, especially the visitor areas. Install more cameras, hire more personnel. Pay closer attention to who's coming onto the property. No one that we don't know gets anywhere near the house. What about attack dogs?"

"Uh..."

"Never mind. We can hold off on that for now. But find out where we can get an armored car in a hurry. I mean fully decked out. Better than whatever the Secret Service has."

"Better than the Secret Service?"

"And I need you to call the airport and have the plane gassed up, since we'll be leaving tomorrow morning. And if you can—"

"No, we're not," Frankie's voice calls out behind me.

"Hang on," I tell Armani, turning to face my wife.

She's standing in the bedroom doorway, wearing the FBI shirt with the skirt half of her waitress uniform sticking out the bottom.

"Or at least, *I'm* not leaving tomorrow," she says, crossing her arms over her chest.

I frown. "Armani, why don't you go ahead and start marshaling the troops. I gotta go. Talk soon."

I hang up without waiting for his reply. As I get up and move toward Frankie, I realize that her expression is standoffish and cool. Whatever connection we had last night seems completely gone. Does she really think I came all this way only to leave without her?

"Listen," I say gently. "I know it seems like things are moving really fast, but we need to be back in California as soon as possible so that we can—"

She closes her eyes as if I'm giving her a headache. "You're not *hearing me*, Dante. I live here now. With my mother. My life is here."

I scoff. She's being ridiculous. "And that makes you happy?"

She glares at me. "It makes me *free*."

Involuntarily, I take a step back. It's almost as if she's slapped me. That...really hurt. More than it should have.

"You don't need to be 'free,' Francesca. You're my wife. You're going to be a mother. To my child. You have responsibilities, obligations. But believe me, your safety and comfort are my top priorities, and—"

"I've already called an Uber," she interrupts. "The Jag is still at the diner, so thanks for that."

She grabs her purse from a side chair, slipping the strap over her shoulder as she stalks toward the door. I feel like I should do something to stop her, but I can't move.

Turning back toward me, door handle in her grip, she adds, "And damn it all, my first responsibility is to *myself*. I've let the men in my life absolutely ruin it and I'm DONE. So please, do kindly fuck off."

All I can do is watch in stunned silence as she whips the door wide open and leaves.

Yesterday, she gave me the best possible news I could have ever imagined—and today, she's stormed back out of my life. Fuck. This little Florida experiment has run its course. She's my wife and she's coming home where she belongs. I can't keep her safe if she's this far away, and now that she's pregnant, it changes everything.

I grab my phone and dial Armani.

It's time to stop playing nice.

9

FRANKIE

Fucking Dante. What exactly do I owe him?

It's the question I keep mulling over after I leave the diner and take the Jaguar for a long drive on the Venetian causeway, attempting to clear my head. The bridges and bay views always calm me down. The sun and wind are just right, too, and for once I don't feel like I'm suffocating from the weather.

My life seems determined to smother me no matter which way I turn, but I'm not going to let it. I can't. For once, I just want to feel like I'm not trapped. Like I get to make my *own* choices, determine my *own* fate.

Yes, Dante has a right to know his child and be a part of that child's life. That's not up for debate. But he doesn't have the right to dictate every aspect of how I live *my* life. I'm tired of the secrets and half-truths and flat-out lies. The manipulations and ultimatums. I deserve better than that, and so does our baby. So I'll just have to figure out how we're going to co-parent if we're not in the same city, much less the same state. It can be done. I'm determined to find a way.

As for right now, I need to take things one day at a time. That's all I can do. Tomorrow, I'll look for a new job. A more professional one that will actually pay me decent money. See, things are looking up already. And baby bean seems to be letting me keep down the burger and fries I've been eating on the drive, so progress! Though I really should start eating better. And I will.

By the time the sun begins to set, I'm not exactly settled, but at least I'm feeling like I've got a grip on my emotions. I've got this. I'm going to be okay. And I'm ready to head home.

When I pull into the apartment building's rear parking lot, though, the first thing I spy is Dante's rental car in one of the visitor spaces. Instantly, my good mood shatters. Fucking bastard. What the hell is he doing here? I only just got a handle on things, and now this.

Didn't I make myself clear this morning? Yet here he is, obviously planning to strong arm me into doing whatever he wants. He probably figures he'll get my mom on his side, the two of them coaxing me into taking the easy way out—the gilded cage—for the good of the baby.

This is too much.

I sit in the car for a minute, steeling myself for the confrontation that I don't want to have, giving myself a pep talk about how I'm not going to back down. Then I force myself to get out and march to the apartment. Turning my key in the lock, I take a deep breath and then push the door open.

A strange hush goes through the air as I walk inside. And do a double take. No...THIS is too much.

"What the hell?" I blurt.

Charlie, Mom, and Livvie are sitting on the couch. Dante and Clayton are opposite them, in the armchairs, while Armani stands hovering behind Dante. Miggy jumps up when he sees me and bounces over, barking a hello while pawing at my feet.

I don't get a moment to recover from the shock of seeing my family before Charlie and Livvie fly across the room and wrap me in a huge hug, both of them babbling excitedly about my pregnancy.

"This is going to be amazing," Charlie murmurs into my ear. "I promise."

"I can't believe the good news!" Livvie squeals.

"You're going to be a mama! Why didn't you tell us we're going to be aunties?"

I glance past Charlie's head and shoot an evil look at Dante, but he just tilts his head toward my mom, who looks sheepish.

"I um, wanted the time to be right," I say lamely. "But wait...what are you all doing here?"

"It's Thanksgiving! What better time for the whole family to be together?" Charlie says with strained mirth.

Uh-oh. I know that voice. It's the Dad Did Something Again voice.

Our mother scoffs. "Cut the crap. We just need to talk about what's going on. And Livvie deserves to know the whole truth—she knows most of it already, and trying to keep it a secret almost let something bad happen to her, didn't it?"

My stomach drops, and I pull away from my sisters. "*What?* Livvie, what happened?"

"You should sit down, Frankie," Charlie says.

She and Livvie exchange a glance and my heart picks up double time.

"I don't want to sit down. Just tell me. Somebody say something," I demand.

Well, there goes my peace of mind. The hush that's fallen over the room suggests that whatever I'm about to find out is pretty bad.

Charlie clears her throat and gazes at me with clear eyes, using her calmest voice to say, "Two days ago, the last day of school before the holiday break, the vice principal at Livvie's school—Mr. Matthews—noticed two men watching her from the parking lot while she was waiting for the bus. When they got in their car and followed the bus, he followed them."

My hand goes over my chest, where I can feel my heart pounding behind my ribs.

"He wasn't totally sure at first," Charlie goes on, "but when it was clear they really were following Livvie, he called the police to send a cruiser to Bellanti Vineyards. It was enough to scare off the men, apparently, and since there was nobody at the house except the Bellantis' staff, Mr. Matthews drove her to Nob Hill to stay with me."

I glare daggers at Dante just as he rises from his chair and moves toward me. I'm fucking furious. "You didn't even *think* about Livvie and her horses, did you? She rides every single day! Did you seriously think she wouldn't need someone to—"

"Marco was home," Dante says, cutting me off. "It was bad timing. He'd been called away for an emergency; one of the workers broke their ankle in a gopher hole on the grounds."

It's like a record scratch in my brain. "The winery has *gophers*? Have you tried—"

"Frankie, focus!" my mom says.

"Right. Sorry." I turn back to Livvie and take her hand.

She hesitates and then says, "There's more. When we got to Nob Hill, Mr. Matthews said it looked like we were being followed again. So I called Clayton to come out and meet me at the car so he could walk me into the house. He said I needed to get out of California right away, so he used his connections with the Frisco family to get me here without anyone knowing."

"Which is great," Dante cuts in, shooting Clayton a look, "if we're assuming it's not the Friscos who were after her."

Clayton raises an eyebrow in response, which is apparently all that's needed to settle that suspicion. Dante nods at him. It's not the Friscos.

"Why was this Mr. Matthews paying so much attention to Livvie?" Mom asks, showing more maternal concern than she has in the past decade.

Oh, wait. She's nice now. I have to keep reminding myself of that.

"I, um, asked him to keep an eye on her," I admit. "We Abbotts don't exactly have sterling examples of father figures in our lives. Mr. Matthews used to be a counselor when I went to Napa High, and I thought he could be a positive influence. Someone to confide in, if need be."

"Oooh," Livvie says, visibly relaxing. "I was wondering why he called me into his office to offer me counseling. We did talk a few times. He was actually really helpful."

"Good," I say, nodding. "He was always decent to me."

Livvie smiles. "He made me realize some things about my life. And how I was coping in some unhealthy ways—like working until I drop every single day. So...we worked on making a list of some more helpful coping mechanisms I can try. Like watching *Gilmore Girls* and perfecting my peanut butter cookie recipe. Stuff I can do without pressuring myself."

"Oh, Livvie." I can't help wrapping my baby sister in a hug.

The men aren't listening to us anymore—they've launched into planning mode.

"Livvie needs to be hidden. That much is clear," Clayton is saying.

"Not just her," Dante says. "All of the women."

"The whole family," Armani agrees.

Realistically, I know they're right. My fears have come true. We really are in danger.

But I immediately think of the Friesians, and

Livvie's unbreakable bond with them. "What about Livvie's horses?" I ask, interrupting the conversation going on across the room.

The men stop talking to look at me as if I've lost my mind.

"I know it might seem like the last thing we should be thinking about when it's obvious someone is out to get us, but they're important to my sister, so they're important to me," I say firmly.

"Actually," Livvie cuts in, "I think...I think I'm going to take a break. Just for a little while. The show circuit is done until March, and Max and I could probably use some downtime. I can get Vicente to look in on them. He's great with Max. Um, if that's okay with you all."

A murmur of agreement goes through the men. Well, that definitely makes things easier.

"When you say we need to be hidden, what are we talking about? All of us sent away?" I ask.

Dante moves beside me and despite myself, I find comfort in his closeness. "I think for now, it makes the most sense to get Livvie into hiding right away. Armani and I have plans to make sure you're looked after at the house in Napa, and we'll do the same for Charlie at her place. It'll be harder for you to be targets if you're not all in one place together."

Mom moves beside Livvie and gently puts an

arm around her shoulders. "I'm not that fond of Miami, and since your father broke all of his promises, I'll risk whatever threats he wants to throw my way in order to go home and be with my girls," she announces. "I know I need to earn my family's trust back, but taking care of Livvie and helping her stay hidden can be part of that."

She holds her chin high, and Dante slowly nods. "Thank you for the offer, Miriam," he says. "Livvie? How does that sound? We can always make other arrangements."

Livvie nods almost excitedly. Charlie and I exchange a glance and then shrug in agreement. Mom just smiles like she's won the biggest prize. I could get emotional right now, but I hold it back. I'm terrified, yet happy that our mother might be back in our lives again.

"We've got some Frisco connections in New Orleans," Armani says. "They have an old safe house on Lake Pontchartrain. I've been there. It's secluded, easy to guard, and comfortable enough to use long term. The women could stay as long as needed, even Miriam's dog. I'm sure we could arrange for a private tutor to help Livvie finish out school."

Livvie's eyes go wide. "You think it'll be that long? I—I can't be gone for all that time."

"I'm sure it won't be that long," Charlie says

soothingly. "This is all going to get sorted out before you know it."

I stare hard at Dante over Livvie's shoulder as I give her another reassuring hug. "Listen to me, Livvie. I know there's been a lot of broken promises in your life. And I know Dad's done a lot of really shitty things. But I promise you, we are going to find him. And he's going to pay for the damage he's done to our lives."

"It'll be taken care of," Dante says, formally accepting the task I've just given him.

I'm going to hold him to it.

"In the meantime," I tell Livvie, "we need to make sure nothing happens to you. Okay? Baby is going to need their Auntie Livvie."

Just then, there's a knock at the door. Armani motions for everyone to stay where they are. His left hand moves beneath his suit jacket as he strides to the door. The back of my neck tingles when I realize he's reaching for a gun.

I watch him peek through the peephole. "Dinner Dash?" he asks over his shoulder.

"It's safe," Dante calls back.

Armani visibly relaxes, and opens the door to reveal a food-laden delivery person. Clayton moves to help collect bags and boxes, and soon the small apartment smells like a home-cooked meal. After tipping the delivery person, Armani shuts and locks the door.

"Well, Dante. It looks like the feast you ordered could feed this entire apartment building."

Dante shrugs. "I just wanted to be sure there'd be a Thanksgiving for the Abbott sisters. Albeit a few days early.

I look at Dante curiously. "You ordered us Thanksgiving dinner?"

He grins. "Well, it wouldn't be a holiday without turkey, stuffing, mashed potatoes, and gravy, would it?"

Armani pipes up. "Don't forget the pie."

"Looks like there's pumpkin *and* apple." Livvie makes an appreciative sound.

Everyone scrambles to arrange the food buffet-style on my mom's small dining room table. Before long, the feast is laid out with paper plates and plastic forks. We gather as many chairs around the table as we can. Armani even drags over the recliner and positions it in the corner of the narrow dining room.

I can't describe the feelings going through me, knowing that Dante arranged this for us, and that all my family is here. The circumstances that got us here might be unfortunate, but having my sisters around is always nourishing for my soul, and I need them now more than ever. And even though I'm terrified of what might happen to Livvie, I feel better knowing that our mother will be with her.

Funny, I never would've felt that way before.

I go into the kitchen for napkins, and Mom follows me in.

"It's okay, Mom, I've got it," I tell her.

She lightly touches my arm and I turn to face her.

"Dante is a good man, isn't he?" she says quietly. "It seems like maybe he just needs a bit of handling."

I huff a laugh, and then sigh. "Yeah. Just a bit."

"For what it's worth, Frankie, he's nothing like your father. But he could run you over. Don't let him."

She lovingly squeezes my arm before going back out into the dining room. Something flips inside of me and in that moment, I feel like the weight I've constantly carried for all these years has lifted. There's still some resentment there, and it's not like everything is perfect.

But I'm surprised to realize that I've honestly begun to forgive my mother.

10

FRANKIE

THERE'S STILL one question that I can't bring myself to ask Dante.

Just one. It shouldn't be hard to spit out. It's the reason I left California in the first place. But maybe I don't want to know the truth. Maybe I've already made up my mind.

Whatever my mental hang up, I can't quite bring myself to ask him about the debt. The measly $286,000 that sealed my fate. I've tried to say something to Dante a dozen times, but each attempt leaves me with the words dying in my throat, before they can even reach my lips.

Sitting in my seat beside him, I brace myself as the plane bounces through some light turbulence. My stomach is quick to retaliate with a burst of nausea, but I'm able to hold it down. This time.

Meanwhile, Dante sits quietly beside me, reading something on his tablet. He's been attentive, polite, and cold. Back to his normal demeanor...except that he's slightly more tolerable than usual. I chalk that up to my pregnancy. Despite his flaws, he seems genuinely excited about the baby and I am grateful for that.

It feels like the weekend we had at the St. Regis and the Alvarezes' bay cottage never even happened. All buttoned up in his suit and tie, he seems miles away from the man who swam naked and made love to me in the October sun. So I spend the entire plane ride home lost in my own thoughts, watching the country slide by far below me.

And yet...

He'd given me and my mom and my sisters our first Thanksgiving together in over a decade. That had to mean something. There had to be some kind of love still between us. Even if he's not acting like it right now.

It certainly wouldn't be the first time he's emotionally walled himself off from me.

When we finally land at the Napa Airport, a wave of heated emotion hits me out of nowhere. My return to California, necessary though it may be for my safety, makes me feel like I've lost a battle. I get out of my seat first and stalk off the plane, not bothering to wait for Dante.

We had to leave the Jag in Miami (Livvie was *ecstatic* to be given the keys), so I'm not surprised to find Donovan waiting for us in a black Escalade. He and Dante share a look as I slide into the back seat. I have no idea what's passing between the two of them, but I'm too tired to care. The sound of my car door closing makes me tense and antsy.

Trapped. I'm trapped in this SUV, heading back to the life I just ran away from. Crossing my arms, I lean against my door and rest my head on the window. There's an ocean of space between Dante and me on the seat and I'm both comforted and irritated by it.

Why can't he just—

His warm fingers land on my upper thigh. Some of my anger melts.

The ride to the house is quick. Donovan pulls right up to the front door and my chest tightens as the huge, formal building comes into full view. It's so big, so vast, and so...oppressive.

"Here we are," I say, faux-cheerfully. "Back at the mausoleum."

Dante is about to open his door but pauses to glance back at me. "What's the matter?"

"Oh, nothing. Just jazzed to be coming home to this huge, dark, depressing crypt."

The words snap out of me, and for the first time since we left Miami, his expression turns into a frown, as if I've hurt him.

I huff out a sigh. "Sorry. I've had a short fuse for a while now."

"Don't blame yourself," Dante says gently. "I'm sure it's just baby hormones."

My eyes narrow into a death glare. "Get bent."

With that, I slide out of the car and slam the door behind me.

Donovan takes my bag from the trunk, but I snatch it from him—because I can fucking handle it myself, goddammit—and head up to the front door. Dante rushes up behind me, but I keep a steady pace. I don't want to walk into this house, but I have to get it over with. It's like ripping off a Band-Aid. Fast and steady, deep breath, and get it done.

Pushing open the door, I don't stop as I head for the stairs and start lugging my bag up.

"Frankie, let me take that," Dante calls after me.

"I can do it myself, thank you."

He follows me up the stairs, but when I get to the top, I hesitate. His room, or mine?

Suddenly, his arms wrap around me possessively from behind, one hand resting on my belly. My heart flutters as his lips brush the sensitive skin behind my ear.

He takes my bag and nudges me toward his room —our room—and I don't bother putting up a fight, thanks to him kissing my neck until I'm breathless. Desire floods my veins, my resistance and irritation beginning to wane. I've used sex to get Dante to open up before. Maybe that's the key. For the sake of the little lima bean, I need to make this work.

And if it doesn't…at least I'll be getting some.

Dante steers me into the bedroom, setting my bag next to the closet, leading me toward the bed.

"I need to take a bath," I mumble as he spins me in his arms to face him.

"After. This first."

His lips claim mine and there's no protesting as his tongue darts into my mouth. Wrapping my arms around him, I sigh as he lifts me in his arms and carefully sets me on the bed. My head begins to spin with lust, the sweet, addicting kind that takes me out of my head and far from reality, so I feel nothing but the pleasure of his touch.

He makes quick work of our clothes, and as my eyes rove his naked body, I instantly forget about the bath—all I want is to feel him deep inside me. But Dante has other plans. Spreading my legs wide, he settles between them to pleasure me with his tongue, his lips, his thick fingers, so I just close my eyes and sink into the firestorm of sensations he's drawing out of me. It's one hit of pleasure after another, lifting me higher, making me float and dip and spiral.

And need.

My fingers dig into his hair as he finally moves over my body, and his cock gliding into me feels like coming home. His name bursts from my lips again and again as he pushes me into a blinding orgasm. Everything feels right in that moment—a sense of peace and perfection pumping through me as I ride the waves of pleasure.

The next thing I know, the blankets are pulled up to my chin and then I hear the sound of water running from the en suite. The lush scent of cherry blossom fills the air, making me smile as I sit up. Dante comes out of the bathroom, his arms loosely crossed as he watches me.

"Your bath is ready. I'll have some food brought up while you're soaking. Tea?"

"Yes, please."

Just like that, I feel cared for again.

By the time I slide into bed next to Dante, I'm warm, full and...content. With his arms wrapped around me, a dreamless sleep comes fast, but so does morning. I'm a little disoriented as I blink groggily at the sun-soaked room, lying in a bed that's both familiar and strange.

It's Dante's bed. No—our bed. In our room. Home, in California.

Unfortunately, a glance at the clock tells me I've slept way later than I intended. I need to get to the tasting room. Try to give this life of mine some sense of purpose and accomplishment. Dante had been insistent that I don't have to work if I don't want to, but it only confirmed that he still doesn't understand me as a person. Luckily, there's just over an hour until the first tasting of the day, so I still have time to get ready. I practically leap out of bed.

I wash my face and pull back my hair, then throw on some light makeup, all while trying my best to hold back the familiar nausea that plagues me every morning. Opening the closet, I'm relieved to see that all my designer clothes are still here. I pull out one of my favorite skirt suits and quickly get dressed. I'm aware it's at risk of getting barfed on if I'm not careful, but I won't be able to fit into it for much longer, and dammit I want to look good for my first day back.

After a brief stop in the kitchen for a hug from Alain and a bland (but fairly safe) late breakfast of oatmeal, a special blend of ginger and peppermint tea, and toast, I call the Bellanti offices and leave a brief message with Ruby to let Dante know I'll be in the tasting room for the next few hours. The last thing I need is for him to go ballistic because he can't find me. When I step outside the front door, I find Donovan waiting for me.

"Morning," I say. "Are you my personal guard?"

He merely nods, escorting me silently to the winery.

My spirits are lifted by the time I walk into the tasting room, leaving Donovan at a small corner table where he can keep an eye on me for the duration of my shift. Some of the staff bombard me right away, inquiring about how my sick mother is doing. It takes me a second to realize that must be the story Dante gave everyone to cover for my sudden disappearance.

I assure them that she's making a rapid recovery, and that the doctors say she'll be back to her old self in no time. Honestly, I feel bad every time I have to lie to a coworker, but the truth isn't for them to know.

Speaking of my mother, the tummy tea recipe she'd sent to Alain for me really seems to be doing the trick. I'm a little queasy off and on during my shift, but by the time I'm ready to clock out, the bean hasn't rioted out my breakfast. I'll have to call my mom later and thank her.

That stops me in my tracks. I can just...call my mom. What a concept.

There's a smile on my face as I collect Donovan

and let him know I'm heading to the Bellanti offices next, to go over some new purchase orders.

"You're more than welcome to wait for me in the lobby," I tell him. "Or if you want to be closer to my office, I'm sure Ruby wouldn't mind the company."

"I can sit with Ruby," he says.

I swear I see Donovan's cheeks turn the slightest hint of pink.

But a few steps into the building, my ears are assaulted by the foul, familiar sound of Jessica's distinctively fake, overly sweet laughter coming from one of the offices down the hall.

Oh, hell no.

Bitterness wells in my throat, the tummy tea suddenly losing its effect.

I keep walking, but my mood is ruined.

Fucking Jessica.

I can't believe that bitch is back. The memory of seeing her through the window on her knees, licking her lips like a satisfied cat, has my stomach clenching. Good. If I'm going to throw up, it's going to be right on top of Dante's double-crossing desk.

Marching into my husband's office, I slam the door behind me.

Dante looks up, startled, as I cross my arms and lean back, jutting out a hip.

"You are *such* a massive fuckwit."

11

FRANKIE

Dante is about to rise from his chair, but I stop him with a hand in the air.

"Seriously? I'm fucking pregnant, and you still have her dangling?"

He shakes his head, as if he actually doesn't know what I'm talking about. "Who?"

"Jessica!" I shout, then lower my voice to a hiss. "Unless you have another sidepiece I don't know about."

"*Jessica?*" he repeats, acting like he's confused. "I haven't even thought of her that way since—"

"Oh no? You don't think about the woman who sucks your dick during the workday?" The volume of my voice is kicking up again. It's taking all my will not to scream at him.

"Frankie, what the hell are you—"

"I heard you! The two of you. In the front room, at the house. She was on her knees sucking you off and you called her beautiful in Italian and I SAW her wipe her filthy mouth—"

"It wasn't me," Dante says as he gets up, raising his hands in an attempt to placate me.

"Yeah, I've heard that song before," I scoff, backing away.

My cheeks are flaming hot, the burning in the base of my throat almost suffocating. I need a drink. I need my damn tummy tea.

"I don't know what you saw or heard, but it wasn't me," he repeats. "Swear to God, I don't know what you're talking about." He edges around the desk cautiously, like I'm a terrified deer that he's going to scare off. Right now, I'm a goddamn lioness and he'd better watch out.

"Why should I believe you? You've lied to me before."

Dante's eyes narrow. He's losing patience, I can tell, but I don't care. Jessica shouldn't be here. She should have been fired and gone. Oh wait, she *had* been fired and gone, but for some reason she's back now. She's always back.

"Frankie, I haven't touched another woman since we were married. That's the honest truth."

God, he sounds so sincere. I want to believe him. But I don't know if I can.

He's come completely around the desk, his body mere inches from mine. I look into his eyes, searching for any hint of deceit. My pulse ticks up as my anger begins to fade.

Seeing me waver, Dante pulls me close by degrees, inch by inch, giving me an out if I want one. But I let him gather me against his chest, my hands sliding around his back. I don't want an out. I just want...reassurance. The kind I can trust.

Nuzzling my ear, he murmurs, "Listen to me, please. I swear on my life—on our child's life—that I've been faithful to you. Even when I thought our marriage wasn't legal. Because I still loved you. And I still do."

"Then who was it? And why is she still here?" My anger has lost its momentum and my voice is weak. I don't believe he's lying.

He tips my chin up with the warm press of his finger. We lock eyes and his thumb brushes my lips, sending a hot pulse straight between my legs.

"I don't know, but I'll find out. And I'll take care of it. Francesca, I promise you, I—"

Someone knocks on the door and then it bursts open. Marco saunters in, clueless as always, then spots us embracing and has the grace to look embarrassed. For a second.

"Welcome back, Frankie," he says.

I pull back from my husband, who is shooting a death glare at his brother.

"Thank you."

He winks at Dante and runs a hand over the back of the leather chair near the desk. "Do you have anything going on this afternoon?" he asks me.

"Um, not really—"

"Good, good. See, I was wondering if you'd want to lead the afternoon tour for me, because I have this...thing that I need to do, and maybe you can cover for me, pretty please?"

I can't help but laugh at the way Marco's batting his lashes at me, his hands clasped to his chest in supplication. Even though I'm more than sure that this urgent "thing" that he has to do probably involves women, fast cars, or both.

"Seriously, Marco?" Dante exhales loudly, annoyed. "She's not back a full day yet and you're already having her do your job?"

"Wow, Dante, you almost made a joke," Marco says with a grin. "Damn, Frankie, you are good for him. Way to lighten his ass up. And thanks for covering me. I owe you one. And, ah, don't wait dinner on me."

Marco shoots us finger guns and then spins out the door, kicking it closed behind him.

"You *are* good for me," Dante says.

"Did he just air gun me?" I say.

Dante pulls me against him. "I'm going to do more than air gun you. That's a promise."

He kisses me. And then again, longer this time. Long enough that I'm out of breath when he's done, my knees weak. The third kiss is even deeper, even more mind-bending as his lips take mine, little moans escaping my throat. Pushing me gently backwards, he walks us over to the door, where he reaches around me to flip the lock.

The sound goes straight to my core, filling me instantly with a hot rush.

Wrapping my arms around his neck, I kiss him back, hard and aggressive, with all the passion his lips are giving me. My hands slide down to tug at his belt, but I'm so needy and impatient that I can't get the buckle to loosen. When I let out a groan of frustration, Dante chuckles against my mouth and moves us to the couch.

He sits down first, working off his belt and then sliding his pants down for me. His cock is ready, hard and thick, throbbing as I grip it with one hand. I let him pull me down onto his lap, ruck up my skirt, and push my underwear to the side. His fingers skim the wetness between my legs, tracing my lips before he gives my clit the softest pinch.

"Mmm," I moan, squeezing his dick in response.

A bead of precum slicks the tip, and I use my thumb to swirl it around the sensitive head and down the shaft, the moisture just enough to provide the lubrication I need to lightly pump my fist around him.

His head falls against the back of the couch. "Fuck, Frankie."

Still stroking him, I lean forward, balancing myself on the couch on one knee so I can straddle him properly. His hands grip my hips and move me into position over him, his erection pulsing hot at my entrance.

Our eyes lock, and we watch each other as I slide down onto his cock, both of us groaning softly as I sink deep. My hands move to clasp his tightly, and we kiss softly as we work each other, finding a steady rhythm. Soon we're moving faster, Dante ramming up into me with his pelvis at just the right angle. Sliding a hand between us, he circles my clit with his thumb, igniting the sensitive nerves there, and the dual touch sends me straight over the edge. Burying my face in his neck, I muffle the groans of my release. Dante lets out a gasp, panting my name, his hands suddenly grabbing my ass tight as he thrusts up once, twice, and explodes inside me.

Our tandem breathing is so loud in my ears, I'm sure the whole office can hear. But I can't bring myself to care. I just want to stay curled against him here forever.

He finally shifts me gently beside him and pulls a clean handkerchief from his pocket.

"See, you really are good for me," he says, handing it over. "You got me to take a break in the middle of a workday."

Shaking my head playfully, I clean myself up and straighten my clothes. He's just finished getting himself back together as another knock sounds on the door, followed by the rattle of the doorknob. Obviously, whoever is out in the hall doesn't know what just happened.

He glances at me to make sure I'm all prim and proper again and then waits for me to make myself busy behind his desk before he opens the door.

"Oh—Frankie. Didn't know you were back."

Jessica's disdainful voice coming from the doorway snaps me to attention. Her smile instantly goes from feral and possessive to brittle and forced as I make eye contact with her.

I lean back in Dante's chair, trying to play it cool,

but I can't keep a little smirk off my lips. "I could say the same for you," I say.

Her eyes narrow. "There's a wine tasting starting now. Shouldn't you be going?"

"It's not for another four minutes," I reply breezily. "And Greg's got it. I'm just here signing my VP paperwork."

Her jaw drops, and Dante shoots me an exasperated look.

"V...P?" Jessica sputters.

"That's right," Dante says. "So, if you'll excuse us."

He's backing my story. I can feel a broad smile straining my cheeks.

Jessica's eyes dart between us, and she starts to say something, but then thinks better of it and leaves with a huff, pulling the door shut behind her.

I rise from the desk chair and head for the door myself, stopping to give Dante a well-earned smooch on my way out.

"You're lovely," I tell him. "But you better not make a liar out of me. Go get that paperwork drawn up. VP of Operations has a nice ring to it, don't you think?"

Strutting down the hall, I throw a look over my shoulder to find him leaning out the door, watching me go.

"Francesca Bellanti, you're gonna be the best damn VP of Operations we've ever had!" he calls out, loud enough for the whole office to hear. "Bellanti Vineyards is in good hands!"

"Damn right I will be!" I holler back before rounding the corner with a huge smile on my face.

12

FRANKIE

I'm thrilled to find Charlie and Clayton at the table when I enter the dining room later that night.

A late afternoon toss-all-the-cookies session made me late to the meal I'm not even sure I can keep down, but I doubt anyone will mind, judging by the fact that they're all engaged in a conversation. Dante is so engrossed that he doesn't seem to notice I'm there until I pull out the chair beside him.

"He's hiding out somewhere. I doubt he made it far, not without money. He'd have to be calling on a lot of favors to stay hidden."

"He could be anywhere."

"Unless he's dead."

I look at all the faces around the table, settling on two that I don't know. Men, both of them—and although they aren't wearing uniforms, they have the stiff bearing and broad shoulders of ex-military or police.

"If my father was dead, we'd know about it by now," Charlie says. "Someone would make damn sure we knew."

She puts on a smile when I catch her gaze, but it does little to cover the stress lines between her eyes. Clayton's expression is stony. Armani looks deep in thought, and Marco...he's got the bottle of wine right next to his glass, and it looks almost empty.

"I didn't realize we were having company tonight," I say to Dante, keeping my voice light while cutting my eyes at the two strangers.

He clears his throat and takes my hand. "Francesca, these gentlemen are David Farman, who is now in charge of security for the winery, and Jim Bryant...he's a police officer and an old friend of Marco. Jim's not here in an 'official' capacity."

"Do I want to know what that means?" I say mildly, though my blood pressure is already climbing.

Dante glances at Bryant—who nods—and then back to me. "He's going to help us track down your father. As a favor."

"Do we have to?" I try to joke, but the larger part of me is dead serious.

The food comes out just then, stopping the chatter around the table.

Oh God, no. It smells like veal...and onions. Nope.

Bile lurches into my throat and I shake my head, closing my eyes. Dante has my plate immediately taken away.

"Can I get you something else?" asks Alain's assistant, apologetically.

"I'll just stick with the soup," I tell him. "Thanks."

"You need more than soup," Dante says.

I gesture to my middle. "Tell that to the lima bean."

A few laughs go around the room, followed by the clank of silverware. Everyone takes a few bites and Armani gets the conversation going again.

"Charlie, Frankie: Jim needs a list of every place your father liked to frequent around town. Every bar, racetrack, betting office, or illegal gambling joint you can think of."

"I've already tried all of them, more than once." I break a roll in half and start buttering it, thankful that I can still eat bread without gagging.

"Me, too," Charlie says. "And I talked to everyone I could. Nothing but dead ends."

I snap a look at her. "You shouldn't have done that. It's too dangerous."

She gives me a condescending look. "Seriously?

I'm the big sister. And you went yourself, anyway, so don't be a hypocrite."

My hormones have me instantly on the defensive. "*I'm* a hypocrite? What about the—"

"It's fine that you already looked," Armani interrupts, "but Jim can dig deeper than we can. It would also be helpful to let him know about any friends, known associates, or relatives that your father might have made contact with, especially people who live out of town."

Charlie and I nod, chastened.

"We'll help however we can," I say.

Jim takes out his phone and opens a note app, then looks at me expectantly. A shiver goes through me at the intensity of his stare. This isn't a man who's used to waiting or not being obeyed. Squirming a bit in my seat, it seems like I'm the one under the microscope.

In between bites, Charlie and I list off the places our father liked to hang out. Bars—lots of bars—gambling houses, racetracks, strip clubs, even the all-night-breakfast joints where he'd nurse his hangover with eggs and toast. He doesn't have any real friends, but I'm able to name a few guys he's mentioned over the years, as well as the name of a woman in Reno he used to stay with every now and again, though it seemed like all they'd ever do was drink and fight.

By the time we're done detailing Dad's debauchery, it feels like we've taken a grand tour of indolence and sin.

"What about the tattooed man? The one Bregman claimed ordered the hit?" Dante asks.

Officer Bryant shakes his head. "The description of the suspect's been circulating, but so far it hasn't turned up anything solid. Doesn't mean the guy's not out there, though."

The remainder of the meal is a tense affair, but before anyone has even finished, I realize I've suddenly lost what little appetite I had. I give my sister a look before pushing away from the table and excusing myself. Dante tries to argue, but I cut him off.

"I need some air—I'm going to go check on the horses for Livvie. Don't worry. Donovan will be close by."

"And I'll go with her," Charlie says, excusing herself too.

We link arms and head down the hall to the front door. As expected, Donovan is waiting there like a sentry. He quietly falls into step behind us.

"I can't stomach what else they have to say about Dad," I confess. "Not tonight."

Charlie squeezes my arm. "I'm with you. Come on, let's take some pictures to send to Livvie."

The stables are spotless, warm, and comforting. Delores's son Vicente and the Bellanti stable hands have clearly been taking excellent care of the Friesians, considering how the horses' coats gleam and that the stalls are full of clean straw, fresh food and water, and even toys and salt licks. Livvie couldn't have done a better job herself.

Ytse tosses his head when he hears us approach and buries his warm muzzle in the crook of my arm when I lean over the door of his stall.

Charlie snaps a few photos and texts them over to Livvie.

Opening the door to the gelding's stall, I go in and wrap my arms around the horse's neck. His thick, flowing mane tickles my cheeks while he nickers softly, as if he knows I'm having a hard time. Charlie feeds him a handful of oats and then we sit together in the corner of his stall while he gently nuzzles between us, looking for more treats. Dante would have a fit if he saw me sitting on the ground so close to this massive horse. But he doesn't know Ytse like I do. He's more lapdog than horse.

Charlie plucks straw from her wool pants. "Did Mom tell you anything while you were staying with her? About, you know, when she left?"

I nod, trying to gauge whether my sister wants to

know the truth or if she's asking out of curiosity that doesn't truly want to be satisfied.

"It was...complicated," I admit. "It's honestly not at all what we thought."

She looks surprised at my answer. "She tried talking to me, but I told her I was there for Livvie and that I didn't want to hear it."

"Do you want to hear it now?"

Our eyes catch, a million pulses of our childhood pain going between us. Her voice is quiet as she says, "Yeah. I guess I do."

Taking a deep breath, I take Charlie's hand in mine and haltingly relay the series of events that resulted in our mother's departure from our lives. The abuse she endured from our father, how she'd held out for years hoping he'd change, her eventual decision to divorce him and try to get him to face his addictions. I can barely bring myself to detail what he made her do to settle his debts, the videotape blackmail. Charlie listens silently, her face shut-off and blank.

"He *made* her leave us," I finish. "She thought we were going to live like princesses."

My voice cracks on the last word, and Charlie bursts into tears.

"I knew she loved me," she chokes out between sobs. "I hate him."

"I know," I say gently, rubbing her back. I don't need to ask who she's referring to.

Charlie's tears keep coming, but I just murmur soothing words and let her get it out. She's processing years of buried trauma and pain, the deep wounds suddenly reshaping themselves around these new revelations. I know what she's feeling. I felt the same way.

"He forced her out of our lives, and for what?" she sobs. "For the enjoyment of watching us suffer through our whole childhoods? Or was he just biding his fucking time so he could eventually pimp us out?"

"Knowing him, I wouldn't doubt it." There's no point in sugarcoating it.

A puff of warm air on my leg draws my attention to Ytse. His head is down, his ears forward as if he's listening and sympathizing.

"You know, I saw Mom the night she left." Charlie pats the horse's nose.

"You did?"

She nods. "I got up for something in the middle of the night, I don't even remember what. And I found her in the foyer with a suitcase. She didn't see me at first, but I saw her. She was crying, not making a sound, just standing there. Shaking. And she looked terrified. I don't know, maybe she couldn't figure out whether to stay or just get the hell out of there. But then she saw me. And she just...smiled, like nothing was wrong, and told me this lie about how she needed to go on a business trip. She said she'd be back soon."

My brows knit together. "Mom didn't work."

"Yeah," Charlie says. "The thing that always stuck in my mind is the way she lied to my face. It's like...in that moment, I convinced myself I believed her—I *knew* it wasn't true, but I wanted to believe her, I didn't want her to cry anymore, I didn't want *her* to cry. So I just played along and pretended it was okay. I convinced myself it somehow had to be true. That she'd come back. But she never did.

"God, Frankie, for years I held on to that. How I let her lie to me and just walk right out the door. And I was so angry at her. I had no idea that..."

She starts crying again, which sets me off, and I put an arm around her shoulders and pull her close. We're finally interrupted when Ytse moves closer and noses at Charlie's hair.

"You big monster," she teases, laughing through her tears.

We quiet down, taking turns petting Ytse's nose.

After a moment, I say, "Dad's got a long list of things he needs to pay for, doesn't he?"

Charlie takes a deep breath.

"I hope..." she whispers. "I hope Clayton kills

him. I hate myself for wishing that on my dad, and on Clayton. But...I can't help wanting it all the same. Do you think that makes me a bad person?"

"No," I whisper back. "It makes you human."

I lean my head on her shoulder and hold my big sister close.

13

FRANKIE

Is it too much to hope that my life has finally, finally settled into some kind of rhythm?

Because it feels like it has—and I find myself leaning into the routine. Though admittedly, I'd enjoy it a whole lot more if I didn't have Donovan as my constant shadow, and an army of big burly men strategically placed around the property. But for now, it is what it is. A safety measure, and a mandatory one.

Life is chugging along. I've temporarily given over my wine tastings to Greg, who is really shining in the role. I have my own hands full with the mentorship program I started to put a few of the other employees on the path to their sommelier certification.

It seems like everyone is busy right now. The

winery is flourishing, Dante's schedule is packed every day, and I could certainly take on triple my responsibilities if I wanted to. But at the moment, I like how comfortably full my plate is. Considering I still have to throw up a thousand times a day, I need a little wiggle room for frequent bathroom breaks.

Meanwhile, Marco is working to get Bellanti Racing off the ground. He just got his full competition license and has an important race in Vegas coming up this weekend. It's been causing some very palpable tension between him and Dante. They're arguing about it for what seems like the hundredth time as we sit around the breakfast table.

As I sip my tummy tea, Dante stabs his eggs angrily, spearing Marco with a glare.

"I already told you," Marco is saying, "I'm not canceling the race. It could make or break the team. I've worked way too hard to get us onto the pro circuit to just walk away now."

"You're going to get yourself killed," Dante growls.

Marco smirks. "I refuse to live in fear, Dante. Besides, I'm a damn good driver."

"He's not talking about the driving," Armani cuts in, silencing everyone.

I look around the table. Is Marco in danger, too?

From whom? But I know better than to ask right now. The tension in here is so thick, I can almost taste it.

"Fine, fine, fine," Marco says, holding up his palms. "Look. I will take several of our security people with me, including Farman. Someone will always be watching me, and my car. And if it makes you feel better, I'll have a bodyguard at my side until the moment I get in the car and then immediately after I get out. Okay?"

Dante works his jaw, then continues eating. Armani says nothing. There isn't any further discussion about the matter for the rest of the meal, so I assume Marco will be getting his way.

After the dishes are cleared away, I leave with Marco to visit the private airport in Sonoma.

As Donovan drives us in the Escalade, Marco chats me up in the back seat. I nod along as he tells me about his plans for the racing company—which do sound promising. In fact, the more he talks, the more I start to suspect that on at least some of the nights when he's been presumed to be out partying and bedding women, he's actually been at the garage under the hood of a car.

Eventually, he circles back to Dante. "It's just so frustrating the way he's been fighting me every step of the way. We're doing great on the circuit—and if things continue on this trajectory, we'll be racing with the pros soon. Do you know what it would do for the winery, to have the Bellanti Vineyards logo wrapped all over a winning, professional race car?"

He's right. "That would be unbelievable advertising. Although...I'm assuming that's not the only reason you're doing this."

"It's not." He smiles, showing off that trademark Bellanti masculine beauty. "I do it because it's the only thing that gives my life true meaning."

What can I say to that? Isn't it the same way for my sister and her horses?

Once we're at the airport, Marco brings me to meet Dean Rivers, a pilot interested in starting a helicopter tour company and working in conjunction with the winery. Apparently, Dean has been hounding Armani about the proposal for years, but Armani's been reluctant to consider such a venture. Marco, however, can easily see the potential. Hence this visit.

As Dean walks toward us, I realize he's nothing like I expected. He's older, with an overgrown mop of golden white hair, a thatch of stubble along his jaw, and blazing blue eyes highlighted with deep crow's feet, as if he's spent a lot of time in the sun, or smiling, or both. Probably both. His Hawaiian shirt is faded, and he's...barefoot. If I had to guess, I'd say he's one of those old school, ride-the-wave,

NorCal hippies that never want to give up their youth.

"Hey, man, you finally made it!" Dean says to Marco by way of greeting, flipping back his long hair with a boyish toss of his head. "Man, I've been waiting for this opportunity a loooong time now, you know? Well met, brother, well met."

He gives Marco a half-hug and claps him on the back, then turns to me with a broad grin.

"I'm Frankie," I say, holding out my hand. He takes it in his, giving it a gentle squeeze.

"Dean—it's truly, truly a pleasure to meet you... Mrs. Marco Bellanti, perchance?"

Marco and I both burst out laughing.

"I am Mrs. Bellanti, yes, but Dante's my husband."

"Even better," Dean says, laughing along with us. "I have a feeling this kid here's still too wild to be tied down just yet."

I'll admit, I'm a little skeptical. But then Dean invites us into the hangar, where we sit in his meticulously clean office and listen to an exceptionally solid proposal about the tours. Soon enough, I barely notice the overly long vowels and the constant insertion of "man" into almost every sentence. He clearly knows his stuff.

Dean goes over aircraft specs and fuel prices,

breaking down cost per customer per flight. We hear about conversion rates, which type of marketing has been the most effective historically, and exactly how he would weave his business into the fabric of ours. The more we talk with Dean, the more I realize how smart Marco was to put this idea in motion.

"You know," Marco says. "The helipad at the winery is clear. If you're up for it, Dean, we could do a fly over now?"

"Yeeaaah, man," Dean says. "Frankie? You're welcome to—"

"I'm in," I tell him.

I've never been in a helicopter before, but I don't have time to be nervous or overthink it. The next thing I know, the three of us are climbing into the touring helicopter. Dean gives us a short rundown of what the tour would include as he prepares us for the flight with safety measures and makes sure our seat belts are secure.

My heart lurches into my throat at liftoff, the *whump-whump-whump* of the propeller blades above my head jacking my nerves. But then we're in the air, and the helicopter steadies. The land spreading out beneath us looks incredible. We're *flying*. I let out a laugh of pure joy.

Dean is talking the whole time about his plan for

the collaboration. I'm listening intently while I watch the world race by beneath us.

And then...oh no.

I get the barf bag open just in time.

"Duuude," Dean chuckles. "You nailed it in the baaag. That's impressive. We should take a pic, put it on a shirt."

"Good idea," Marco says. "We could put her photo *on* the barf bags, with a quote about your flying being so smooth, you'll hit the bag every time."

Marco winks at me, but all I can do is puke again while they laugh at my misery.

When I finally run out of hurl, I apologize to Dean profusely, though he insists it's no big deal. I'd had my tummy tea this morning, but I should have brought some with me in a thermos. I'd gotten cocky. Lesson learned.

Luckily, we land at the Bellanti helipad a few minutes later. My face is probably green. Not entirely sure that I can stand on my own, I let Marco help me out of the helicopter. A small crowd rushes out of the offices to see the helicopter—no one was expecting one today, I'm sure—and Dante pushes his way to the front. He glares at the sealed barf bag in my hand, his eyes blazing, but Marco sweeps him into a handshake with Dean, leaving me time to slip away and find the nearest restroom.

Donovan is on me instantly, following like a shadow. I'm too focused on my insides to tell him where I'm going...but then I realize I'm not going to make it anyway. Turning to the row of hedges outside the office windows, I give up whatever is left of my breakfast, hoping no one notices.

When I look up, I see Donovan nearby, pretending to study a tree. Realizing that I'm looking directly at him, he smiles, giving up the pretense. Unspooling a garden hose nearby, he comes over to me and starts washing away the evidence.

"Thanks," I say sheepishly.

"These bushes needed watering anyway," he says.

As he walks me from the main building to the tasting room, I clear my throat and ask, "Any chance you won't tell Dante about this?"

He hesitates. "He cares for you, Mrs. Bellanti. Considering there are men around with bad intentions, I don't think he'd care about any...gardening we need to do."

I nod in gratitude, and then step out on a limb. "What do you know about all the extra security?" I ask, trying to make it sound casual. "If Livvie's out of town, then...why are there still so many guards? And what about Marco? Dante doesn't want him racing in Vegas this weekend, but—"

"That's a conversation for Mr. Bellanti to have with you, ma'am," he says gently.

We step into the tasting room, and the coolness of the air conditioning feels like heaven on my face. "You're a good soldier, aren't you Donovan?"

There's a shuffle behind me. "Are you Francesca?"

Spinning to the unfamiliar voice, I find a striking couple behind me. The man is lean but broad in the shoulders, his dark hair gleaming. The woman on his arm reminds me a little of Charlie with her glossy, straight blonde hair and how well she pulls off casual designer slacks and a blouse. She looks poised yet breezy, as if she just stepped off the page of a fashion magazine.

"Yes?" I answer, glancing back and forth between the couple. "I'm Francesca Bellanti."

Donovan gently takes my elbow in a reassuring gesture. "Mrs. Bellanti, it appears we have a few VIP visitors today. May I introduce Stefan Zoric and his wife Victoria—"

"Tori," the woman says, smiling at me.

"Mr. Bellanti's old friends from Chicago," Donovan finishes.

"Not that old!" Tori jokes, then seems to notice my confusion. "Is it not a good day for a private tasting? Dante extended an offer to us a while back to visit any time. We were in LA for some business and decided to take the weekend to visit Napa. I hope it's not an inconvenience?"

"Oh. Hello. Of course it's not an inconvenience. I'm happy to show you around." I'm smiling now, but I'm still a bit taken aback. It's the first I'm hearing about this. "Please, call me Frankie."

"We've been driving around on our own personal wine tour today, but we just *had* to come see the winery that's causing such a stir," Tori adds. "Is Dante available to join us? He and Stefan haven't seen each other in ages. Fraternity brothers, if you can believe it."

That's when I realize: these aren't mob people. I instantly relax.

"Well," I say brightly, warming up, "I believe my husband is a little tied up at the moment, but I'd love to offer you a private tasting in the Little Cellar until he's free."

"That sounds amazing," Tori says, excitement on her face. "We'd love to, wouldn't we?"

Stefan nods, though he's stoic. Reminds me of my own husband. No wonder they're friends.

"And Donovan," I add, "you're very welcome to join us."

"Thank you, Mrs. Bellanti, but I'm still on the job," he says, gesturing for us to go ahead.

I lead the way to the private cellar. With a little squeal, Tori hooks her arm in mine, surprising me as she falls into step with me. Stefan follows us, with Donovan at the rear.

"I've heard *all* about how incredible Bellanti wine is," Tori goes on. "I can't believe I'm getting a front-row seat to the deliciousness."

Her personality is nothing but bubbles and light, a million miles away from all the darkness and mob business I've been dealing with lately, and I can't help liking her right away.

"Believe me, you're in for a treat," I tell her.

I wish I could taste the wine with them, but maybe a little friendly distraction is exactly what I need right now.

14

FRANKIE

AFTER THE TASTING, Dante appears and helps me give the Zorics an impromptu tour of the winery, after which the glamourous couple head back to their rental car—a luxury convertible, of course—with a few bottles of complimentary wine and promises to visit Bellanti Vineyards again soon.

The work day finished, Dante and I head up to our room to get dressed for the apparently *extremely fancy* dinner party we're hosting tonight at the most expensive Italian restaurant in Napa. This is the first I'm hearing about it.

"And who all is supposed to be there?" I ask as I work on my hair with the bathroom door open. Getting the details out of Dante has been like pulling teeth.

"Just some old friends from out of town," he says vaguely. "Guess I forgot to mention it."

"Mm-hmm," I hum, pushing back a wave of annoyance.

The list of things my husband has been "forgetting" to tell me about lately just keeps growing by the day. And I know for a fact that he doesn't enjoy spontaneity—so a last-minute party like this only adds to my suspicion that these strangers are somehow connected to the mob. Why else would we be bending over backwards to impress them?

Finally satisfied with my French twist, I walk over to Dante so he can zip my dress.

He's fixing his tie in front of the walk-in closet's full-length mirror. He looks dashing, as always, but there's more tonight. The deep silver of his button-down sets off the darker tones in his skin and the flecks in his eyes. He runs his fingers loosely through his slicked-back hair, making the strands less severe while keeping the "don't fuck with me" vibe. His silk suit is impeccable, the color a shade between steel gray and black depending on the light.

All he needs is a fat cigar and even I might be tempted to call him Don. Don Bellanti.

"So what are you thinking about the helicopter tours?" I ask as I turn my back to him. "And what about Dean? I like him. He's actually kind of a genius."

As he zips me up, he says, "The numbers are good. It's a good idea. But you're not going to be the one leading the tours."

I spin around to face him, my rush of excitement dampened by his stipulation. "Why not? We can charge a premium if an actual Bellanti gives the tour. Like a grand per head, minimum—maybe even two, depending on which wines we offer at the tasting."

His fingers trace the straps that crisscross my chest. "Then Marco can do it."

"Marco's building his own life," I say. "He's not going to be at the winery forever."

Dante doesn't budge. "He's part of this family and he'll do as he's told. And so will you."

Heat creeps up my neck. "*Excuse* me?"

His eyes move in the slightest of eye rolls as if he's completely exasperated. I step away as he tries to reach for me.

"You are my wife, Francesca. You're my responsibility to keep safe and I can't do that if you're flying around in a deathtrap all day long. Since you don't seem to have enough common sense to stay on the ground, I'm going to make sure you stay there."

Oh...boy. Pulling a deep breath through my nose,

I cross my arms over my chest and think about what to say that won't result in me totally losing my cool.

"Here's the deal, husband. I can see the twisted love logic you're operating under. But you need to straighten it out before you talk to me like that again, or I'll gladly spend the rest of this pregnancy in New Orleans with Livvie, riding airboats and hunting alligators every day."

Dante is unamused. "Why don't you value yourself?"

"What the hell does that mean?" So much for keeping my cool.

"You're pregnant—yet you were working in a diner, eating garbage food—"

"I only just found out—"

"You could have anything you want, yet you insist on rejecting all of my attempts to make your life easy. You don't have to hustle, Frankie. You don't have to work. Can't you just relax and...be a housewife? Be a mom? What's so wrong with that?"

I silently count to three before I open my mouth again.

"There's nothing 'wrong' with it. For other women." I step closer. "Dante, I *do* value myself. I know what I can contribute to this world. *You're* the one who doesn't see it."

He looks past me and smooths his tie in the

mirror one last time. "We're going to be late," he says, turning on his heel and walking out the door.

Letting out a sigh, I give my reflection one last look. My slinky, pale lavender evening gown—my favorite color—flows over my body like a dream, but I swear I can see the fabric clinging to the tiniest hint of a baby bump across my middle. There's a baby in there. It still surprises me sometimes. I grab my wrap and my handbag and follow my obnoxious husband to the car waiting outside.

THE RESTAURANT HAS BEEN CLOSED to the public, of course, to accommodate our private party. The moment we step inside, I'm overwhelmed by the rich scents wafting out from the kitchen—roasted garlic bread, pesto, something...meaty. Objectively, I know these are mouthwatering smells, but they hit me like an assault. My stomach does an impressive somersault, and I pull my hand from Dante's arm and excuse myself to visit the restroom.

"Don't be long," he warns. "We have people to greet."

Right. Not my top priority. My main focus for the night is to not throw up on anyone important or dangerous.

The posh ladies' room has two stalls with frosted glass doors and an Italian marble double sink with an elaborate Venetian mirror, two additional full-length mirrors flanking it on either side. A diffuser fills the air with some kind of cloying floral fragrance that almost has me spewing before I can safely lock myself in one of the stalls.

I dig out the silver flask of cold tummy tea I brought in my purse and swig half of it down, praying it will work. And fast.

A few minutes later I hear the restroom door open, followed by the click, click of heels on the floor. Finally feeling less nauseous, I screw the top back onto the flask and exit the stall.

The woman turns.

Fucking lovely. It's Jessica, fixing her lipstick in the mirror. Of course. If I do throw up tonight, I vow it will be on this woman.

She raises a brow as she spots the flask in my hand.

"Oh, Frankie. Are things really that bad with Dante?"

"Please do fuck directly off," I tell her as I set the flask on the vanity and wash my hands.

"I'm not going anywhere, *Francesca*," she says in a mocking tone. "My career, my future, is with Bellanti. I've put years of my life into that winery.

And no drunk whore is going to run me off with a bad attitude and some spicy vocabulary."

With that, she gives me a smirk and flounces her way to the door.

"I'm having his baby."

Jessica freezes mid-step. When she turns around, I can clearly see the hurt on her face.

Her eyes drop to the flask. "Well then—"

"It's tea," I cut her off. "For my morning sickness. All day sickness, really. I hear it gets better after the first trimester."

Her resting-bitch face crumples as she blinks rapidly, her eyes going glassy. Good God, is she actually going to cry?

But then her expression smooths out, the fake smile back on her face. She shrugs. "I moved on a long time ago. There're two more, aren't there?"

She opens the door with an exaggerated tug and walks out.

I wait a few seconds before following, wondering what exactly she meant by that. When I enter the dining room, however, I'm slapped in the face with the sight of her hanging all over Marco, who wraps his arm around her as well. Just like that, her meaning is clear. Huh.

Could she have been blowing *Marco* that day at the house? That...actually makes perfect sense. And it also explains why she hasn't managed to stay permanently fired. Huh.

Still. What a bitch.

I don't get time to dwell on it as Dante rises to kiss my cheek and then sweeps me around the room to make introductions. I see Charlie chatting with a few of the other spouses. Meanwhile, Armani appears to be the only man without a companion—he really should have invited Candi—and he looks a little tense. Though I doubt not having a date is the cause.

Soon enough, our group is led outside to the restaurant's courtyard, where a beautifully decorated table sits under a canopy of string lights. The center has a sunken arrangement of running water surrounded by small pools of flame, and several outdoor fire cages throw delicious heat against the early December chill. Slipping my wrap around my shoulders, I'm glad when Dante pulls out a chair for me close to one of the firepits. Everyone else is still mixing and mingling as they stroll around the dramatic, gas lamp-lit courtyard in groups of two and three, drinks in hand. I chat with Charlie for a bit, but then Dante reappears to steal me away. He's in the process of pointing out a few new arrivals who I haven't met yet, but doesn't get to make all the introductions before the first course is brought out and we have to take our seats at the table.

All told, there are seven couples (plus Armani) gathered around the huge table. I'm positioned between Dante and my sister Charlie, Clayton on her other side. Beside Dante are Officer Bryant and his handsome partner. I'm charmed by the warm atmosphere and the glamorous company, even though I've already forgotten the names of the rest of the people closest to us.

Charlie must notice me studying them. She leans over to whisper in my ear.

"Most of these are West Coast family connections, the others are from the Chicago family. Pretty sure that one's wife is an elected official in Illinois."

I take a sip of water and whisper under my breath, "Criminals, senators, mobsters, and princes."

Charlie gives me a confused look.

I laugh. "Never mind. Inside joke."

15

DANTE

I'm pleased. The dinner is progressing nicely.

I wasn't completely sure about this gathering, initially. It was Armani's doing. But I trust my brother with my life, so I didn't question him. He's spent the last hour stoically watching everyone, assessing. Weighing and measuring whether any tensions might get out of control.

They won't. We all have something we need from each other, and there's too much at stake.

Frankie downed a good portion of caprese salad and olives and sliced bread dipped in oil, which was a relief to see. She hasn't been able to keep much food down over the past few weeks, and I'm more used to seeing her push her plate away after just a few bites, but tonight it seems like her stomach is under control. Her cheeks are pink, her eyes bright instead of dulled with impending nausea. She actually looks content. I haven't seen that expression in a while, either.

The waitstaff come around to collect the appetizer plates just as Frankie excuses herself and rises from her chair. Guess I spoke too soon.

I stand up. "I'll come with you."

A line forms between her brows. "I'm fine. I just have to use the restroom."

"I'll wait outside the door for you, then," I tell her.

"But—"

I shake my head to dissuade any arguments and put a hand on the small of her back as we leave the table. The set of her jaw tells me she's annoyed at my concern, but I stay glued to her side as we make our way out of the courtyard. Once we're out of earshot of the guests, she shoots me a glare.

"I've been drinking baby tea all afternoon to prepare for this dinner," she hisses. "It's working, but it comes at a price. This is going to happen like a thousand times a day, and it's really going to cut into your work time if you insist on escorting me to every bathroom break. Why are you being so paranoid?"

I don't want to answer that, so I just gesture for

her to enter the ladies' room and post up outside the door until she comes back out.

"Listen," I say softly, taking her hand. "One of the men was talking about all the problems his wife had when she was pregnant. Gestational diabetes, preeclampsia, some liver thing I'd never even heard of. Her morning sickness was so bad she had to be hospitalized and hooked up to an IV. I'm just worried. This is all new to me, too, and I—want to be there for you."

Her posture softens. She sweeps her thumb over my knuckles.

"I'm fine, Dante. The baby and I are fine. I promise."

I squeeze her hand as we return to the table. I don't miss the daggers Jessica throws my way right before she whispers something to Marco that makes him laugh. When the hell did this little tryst start? I'm going to have to talk to my brother...before he makes a hell of a mistake.

But I have something much more important to attend to first.

I straighten up and smooth my tie with one hand. "Can I have your attention? Everyone."

The head waiter has been anticipating my signal —I *may* have planned this whole thing earlier—and he cues his staff to start bringing around champagne. My guests make sounds of curious delight, except for my wife, who looks up at me with big-eyed worry. She's served a glass of sparkling cider and her lips press into a hard line. I put a reassuring hand on her shoulder.

"As you all know, the Abbott and Bellanti wineries are now joined, and the wines we'll produce next year will be something truly spectacular. But there's another surprise coming even sooner than that, something even more special than the perfect wine."

Raising my glass, I turn to my wife. "I'd like to raise a toast to my wife Francesca and our baby, due late next year."

A broad, genuine smile crosses my face. I can feel it. I usually don't smile like this, but I can't help it right now. Frankie, on the other hand...isn't as pleased. Her expression is murderous, and next to her, so is Charlie's. I don't know why, but I don't have time to ponder it as the table erupts into happy cheers and well wishes, several of the women jumping out of their seats to come around and congratulate Frankie.

The food is served, so I sit back down with a glance at my wife, but she won't even look at me. Easy chatter circles the table as everyone enjoys the meal, but Frankie just pokes at her food. Something is obviously wrong. And whatever it is, it's clear that I caused it this time. But I don't get a chance to speak to her alone, since I'm so busy putting on a show for our guests.

When the meal ends, the maître d' comes out to herd the men to the humidor smoking room for cigars and after-dinner drinks. His jovial voice booms a congratulations as he grips my shoulder and pulls me ahead of the crowd. I don't get another look at my wife as I'm shuffled away, but I hear a staff member inviting the ladies to enjoy the indoor garden and piano bar.

A fat cigar and tumbler of brandy are shoved into my hands the moment I step into the smoking room. I'm surrounded by sweet, heady smoke and the sounds of ice clinking against crystal, more well wishes and chuffs from the men.

"That was some announcement. Congratulations!" One of the men from the Chicago family clasps me on the shoulder. "I understand now why things are so urgent."

I give him a nod and walk away, hoping I can slip out the door and go find Frankie for a few minutes alone, but I don't get far. Clayton, Armani, and Marco are sitting with Dom Frisco—he's our connection from the Chicago family—and Dom makes eye contact with me as he beckons me to join them.

That's my cue to enter the fold and start negotiations. I thought I was prepared for this—it's not the first time I've bartered with devils—but my mind strays to my wife and unborn child. I'd sworn to put dirty work like this behind me. My brothers and I are in agreement that we want out, yet here we are, helplessly reeled right back in.

Taking a deep draw of the brandy so it burns my throat, I saunter to the group and stand with my legs apart, taking up the exact space I dread filling.

Dom salutes me with a glass of wine. It's Bellanti wine, from the selection we had sent over for this dinner.

"No wonder you've seen such success, Dante. Money. Influence. A beautiful wife and a thriving business," Dom says, buttering me up. As if I can't see right through him. "The wine is exquisite. Cheers to your continued good fortune."

Another round of cheers goes through the men. Dom stares at me with a slight grin, reminding me that my "good fortune" hangs in the balance.

"*Grazie*," I tell him. "I'm glad you're enjoying the wine."

Dom gives the red a swish in his glass, watching

it swirl. "I imagine it takes quite a bit of blood, sweat, and tears to create something so good."

"It does." There's an edge to my voice now. I know he wants something.

"You could barter with this nectar of the Gods and get whatever you wanted, yes?"

Snuffing out the cigar in a crystal ashtray on the side table, I toss back the rest of the brandy and set the glass down hard. Playtime is over. "Get to the point, Frisco."

He grins wide and mirrors me as he drains the wine and clunks down the glass. Any pleasantry is gone from his face, replaced by the impudent expression of a thug used to plowing down anyone who doesn't bend.

Unfortunately for him, I've never been very flexible.

Armani stiffens, his hand moving subtly to his waist where he keeps his Glock.

Frisco spreads his hands. "We're all family here. Let's just have a conversation, nice and polite." He looks at Armani, who doesn't move his hand.

"I'm listening," I say evenly. "We're just talking, that's all."

"That's right, that's right. Look, we respect what you boys are trying to do...keep the Bellanti name clean. Go legit. But this mess with your father and the mechanic, well, word's gotten around. You still need us. You still need our muscle, our intel."

He pauses. I don't respond, don't even move a muscle, my eyes boring into his.

Dom shrugs nonchalantly. "And you know, there are things we could use from you, too. Aside from your fine wine, that is."

This is it. This is how they set the hook.

They draw you in with the promise of a favor-for-a-favor, and just when you think you're even, there's just one more favor to honor, one more payback, one more debt to pay.

There's never an out unless it ends with a bullet in your head.

I catch Armani nodding his head slightly out of the corner of my eye, but I don't dare look at him. He and I have talked about this. We knew going back in was the only way to shut down the threat against our family.

Our father's death absolved our ties with the mob. We got a lucky break. But now, here we are, about to retie the knot.

An image of Marco's race car skidding off the asphalt and bursting into flames goes through my mind. Armani, gunned down in broad daylight. And Frankie, she means everything to me...and the baby... they're all in danger. The Bellanti family needs more help that I can provide with my own two hands. I have to protect them.

Sometimes you have to eat the bitter to keep the sweet.

Shoving my hands into my pockets, I square up with Frisco. "What do you need?"

16

FRANKIE

The women are in high spirits, but their joviality doesn't touch me.

The piano bar inside the restaurant is beautiful, with wide windows that must overlook the rolling hills of Napa during the daytime. A wall with etched glass partitions divides us from the men, but I can still make out clouds of smoke swirling on the other side as the men puff their cigars. I can't see them completely thanks to the design in the glass, but I can tell Dante is in there. I'd recognize the set to those shoulders anywhere. He's standing and tense, flaming my fear over what they're all discussing right now.

I should be at Dante's side, not sitting back while he makes decisions that affect the entire Bellanti family—and business—with zero input from me.

He's schmoozing with the *mob*. The very idea terrifies me.

The Frisco wife sits down at the piano and plunks a few keys. Everyone except me is at least a little tipsy by now, and a few of the women start egging her on to play a song. In return, Mrs. Frisco grins and starts picking out notes. It only takes a few bars for everyone to realize she's playing some pop song from the 80's. Maybe the B-52s.

Her technique is flawless, and some of the women gather around the piano and start to choppily sing along. They're all wasted, so the words being sung are mostly wrong, but no one cares. I notice that no one is more animated or friendly than Jessica herself, touching shoulders, throwing her head back in a carefree laugh, acting like she's the life of the party. I refuse to stand here and watch, so I head over to the window to brood.

A moment later, Charlie comes to my side and slips an arm around my shoulder.

"I should be in the smoking room," I tell her. "I know the real reason this dinner happened is going on in there right now. Without me."

I can feel my blood pressure spiking.

Charlie gives me a squeeze. "You'd never be allowed in on it. Trust me. It's just...how it is. Nothing we can do about it."

Clamping my jaw, I don't respond. Anything I could say would only sound hateful, and probably make Charlie feel like I'm judging her for the life she's chosen.

We turn back around to watch the shenanigans going on around the piano.

"Jessica sure knows how to make friends with mob wives," I whisper, watching her ingratiate herself with them like a pro.

"Maybe she *is* a good fit for Marco," Charlie whispers back.

I make a harumph of irritation. I know—I just *know*—that Jessica is waiting for her chance to pounce. And if Marco isn't careful, there's going to be a second pregnancy in the Bellanti family soon... Or maybe she'll just use my morning sickness as an excuse to take more control over the winery's operations. I heard her bragging at dinner about how she was going to be leading the helicopter tours—she's sure to claw her way in further as soon as she can. And then there'll be no hope of ever getting rid of her.

Just then, the double doors open and the men file in, bringing a thick fug of rich cigar smoke with them. I'm instantly queasy, but I try to ignore it and look like I'm having a good time as Dante makes his way to me. He's smiling, his posture more relaxed. It's clear that whatever business was supposed to take place tonight is now over and that the evening is beginning to wind down. I want to ask Dante what happened, but I don't get the chance before more commotion takes place at the piano.

The Frisco woman's husband takes a seat beside her on the bench and whispers in her ear, drawing a loud laugh out of her as she shakes her head. He cajoles her with a bit of soft encouragement, the group of women joining in, and soon enough, Mrs. Frisco agrees.

"Fine! I guess since we warmed up with "Rock Lobster," I might as well put my voice to use," she says. "I suppose we could try something a little more...fitting for the occasion."

It strikes me as a bit of an act, something she and her husband must have rehearsed or at least discussed. A round of light applause goes around, along with a few whistles and catcalls. When the waitstaff suddenly enter the room, setting out chairs in a semi-circle around the piano for everyone to sit in, it's clear this whole thing was a planned part of the night all along.

Mr. Frisco strikes a dramatic chord, and his wife takes a deep breath. When she starts to sing, her voice strong and melodious, the opening notes stun me a little. I shift uncomfortably in my seat as I recognize the aria. It's in Italian, from *Don Giovanni*. And it is breathtaking.

It's also a song I'd hoped to never hear again.

"In what abysses of terror, into what dangers,
Your reckless path pursuing,
Have guilt and folly brought you!
The wrath of heaven will surely overwhelm you,
It is swift to destroy.
The lightning flash of retribution impending,
It will soon be upon you!
Eternal ruin at last will be thy doom. Wretched Elvira!
What a tempest within thee, thy heart divideth!
Ah, why is there this longing? These pangs of sorrow?

Cruel heart, thou hast betrayed me,
Grief unending upon me he cast.
Pity yet lingers, I'll not upbraid you,
Never can I forget the past, the happy past.
When my wrongs arise before me,
Thoughts of vengeance stir in my breast,
But the love that at first he bore me,
Binds my heart to him at last."

It's Elvira who's singing—Elvira who loves the murderous Don Giovanni, despite his evil ways. The last time I heard this, I was with Rico in Italy, at the Roman Arena di Verona. It had been the most romantic night of my life then. The next day, he'd proposed.

The lyrics, the story, the memory...they slam into me, instantly overpowering me. Tears sting my eyes and start spilling down my cheeks. Dante tries to pull me close, but my stomach lurches at the scent of smoke still clinging to him.

I have to get out of here.

Whispering to Dante, I excuse myself without an explanation and beeline for the door. Out in the front foyer of the restaurant, I find Donovan along with a handful of other men—clearly all bodyguards—who snap to attention as I make my way over.

Donovan rushes to my side.

"Mrs. Bellanti?"

"Please take me home now. I'm not feeling well."

He glances around, hesitating.

"Fucking take me home or I'm calling an Uber!" I snarl, swiping at the mascara leaking from the corners of my eyes.

"It's okay, Donovan. We're leaving." Dante appears behind me and ushers me toward the exit.

When we get to the Escalade, I block his hand before he can grab the door handle.

"*I'm* leaving. You and your rank cigar ass are not."

I fling the door open and climb inside. When Dante moves to get in with me, I block him, throwing out a hand.

"I mean it! Dante, I swear to God, I will puke on you. You fucking reek. Ride with one of your brothers."

His brows drop. "You're serious?"

"As a fucking heart attack."

He opens his mouth to argue but clearly thinks better of it, and with a nod to Donovan, he closes the door for me and steps back onto the curb.

I'm grateful for the quiet on the ride home. I keep the windows cracked to let the cool night air circulate, and Donovan says nothing as he drives. After a heartfelt apology for biting his head off back at the restaurant, which he graciously accepts, I let out a deep sigh and let my head fall back on the headrest.

At least I found out Jessica hadn't been sucking my husband's cock that day. Thank heaven for small victories, right? Otherwise...the rest of the night seems like a total wash.

I'M in bed with my back to the bedroom door and the covers pulled up to my chin when Dante finally comes home later that night. I close my eyes and pretend I'm asleep, but he pads softly across the floor and goes directly into the bathroom.

The shower runs for a while, then turns off. My body is tense while I listen to him moving around on the other side of the bathroom door. I'm on edge. Anger has been churning inside me for hours now. I can't stop thinking about the mob men and what happened in the humidor. What it might mean for our future.

Dante comes out of the bathroom and stands at the foot of the bed. Keeping my eyes closed, I hope that he'll give up on me and just go to sleep.

"I know you're not asleep. And I know you're pissed. Look at me, Frankie."

Fuck.

With a sharp exhale, I roll to a sitting position and stare him down. He's toweling his hair dry, standing there stark naked. And yes, he looks good enough to eat. Bastard.

"You missed your calling as a detective, Bellanti," I spit out at him.

He doesn't bat an eye as he tosses his towel onto a chair. "I don't want to fight."

"Then don't fight me," I snap.

"Francesca, there are things going on that you don't understand. That you can't—"

"No, Dante. There are things going on that I don't *know about*. There's a difference. You're making shady deals in literally smoky back rooms with shady mob people. I understand that much. Now I need to know why."

His eyes shift to the side, his head tilting, and he looks like he's actually considering it.

But then, "I don't want to worry you with—"

With a frustrated groan, I whip the covers over my head and roll onto my side again, back facing him. Undeterred, he slips under the sheet to sidle up behind me, wrapping me in his arms.

I try to stay frozen still as Dante gathers me against him, the warmth of his growing erection pressing into my ass. He threads his fingers through my hair, drawing tingles over my scalp. It's hard to be mad when he's tantalizing me like this, but I'm determined not to waver.

"I didn't make any deals with them," he says, speaking softly into my hair. "I swear. But know this. I'd make a deal with God, the devil, *and* his sister to keep you and this baby safe."

He kisses the back of my neck, trailing his lips to my shoulder as his hand moves to the front of my stomach and tenderly cups my belly. "You and this kid are what matter most to me. I love you, even when you don't love me back."

I think about the song the Frisco woman sang tonight, about Elvira—a woman doomed to love an evil man. I think of the evil things my father did to my mother, to me and my sisters, and was still trying to do. An equally evil person killed Dante's father. But...Dante isn't evil. Sometimes he doesn't do good things, but he's still far from the evil I've experienced in my life.

Turning in his arms, I stare into his eyes.

"I do love you," I tell him. "It makes me *so mad* sometimes, but I do. Please don't doubt that."

Dipping his head, he pulls me close, as tightly as he can, and kisses me deeply. The hem of my shortie nightgown is already slid up, and I lift it to my waist as I throw a leg over his hip and start grinding slowly over his cock. He groans as I move faster, moaning softly in his ear, until finally I can't wait any longer.

I reach down, tug my panties to the side, and draw him into my wetness. He gives a few thrusts, making me gasp, and then I shift, rolling on top of him, spreading my knees wide so he fills me to the hilt. Leaning forward, I drop my lips onto his, our bodies pressed chest to chest.

"Say it," he demands, pulling back to watch me ride him.

"I love you."

I'm out of breath already, my hands going for his shoulders, his biceps, his chest, his abs—anything I can hold on to while I toss and sway over him, desperate to get myself off.

"Again," he says, grabbing my hips to steady me, grinding me even faster against him.

"Fuck." I can barely keep my eyes open from the building pleasure. "I *love* you."

"Again."

"I love you, I love you, I love you," I moan out.

"Don't stop."

So I don't...until our breathing runs together and he's spilling inside me and I'm clenching around him, hot tears in my eyes, giving myself up completely as I'm swept up in his love.

17

FRANKIE

There's a valley that overlooks the Abbott vines that has never lost its magic for me.

It's Monday and the winery is closed, giving Charlie and me the perfect opportunity for a late morning horseback ride. So we saddled up Ytse and one of the mellow winery horses and now we're on a slow, ambling ride up to the little valley inset above the property. The stark blue skies and winter sunshine are a much-needed peaceful break from the craziness of our lives. I try to pretend I don't notice Donovan following us from a distance in one of the vineyard's UTVs, which is basically a tricked-out golf cart that can tackle rugged terrain.

My father had considered planting vines here years ago, since there are a couple of acres of decent soil, but the surrounding hills keeps the area from getting enough sun to produce well. Which was a blessing in disguise, because it meant this land could remain a wild meadow, dotted with a few scrubby oak trees. It's one of my favorite places on the entire property—and one I've come to many times when I needed to be alone.

"How did baby like their first horseback ride?" Charlie asks as she dismounts.

I smile. "Aww, I hadn't thought of that. Baby's first ride. I'd say baby is a natural."

We take in the view and stretch our legs for a bit, giving the horses a chance to rest.

The normally vibrant green of the land is now muted shades of winter brown, but the view is still stunning. Even Charlie comments on how still beautiful it is here.

Settling ourselves down on a smooth boulder under some trees, we dig into the small bag of snacks Alain packed for us before we left—pistachios, red grapes, pretzel snaps, and cheese cubes. We brought water bottles too, but mine is filled with tea.

"I'm still pissed Dante announced your pregnancy at dinner like that," Charlie remarks. "He obviously doesn't know the rules."

"Pff. Not to mention," I add, "why tell a room full of strangers? It's private. I would have at least liked to be able to discuss it with him beforehand. I would've tried to talk him out of it."

Charlie flashes a wry smile. "Which is probably *exactly* why he didn't tell you his plan."

I nod. "Yeah. It's too early to be making announcements. If anything were to happen…"

"Don't even say it," Charlie interrupts. "But yeah…that's why people usually wait until after the first trimester is over. If not longer."

She looks out at the view, going quiet. I don't need to ask what she's thinking about. She and Clayton have been trying to have a baby for years. My sister has miscarried twice, both times in the second trimester, and knows all too well what it feels like to share the happy news, only to be heartbroken later. I've actually been meaning to talk to her alone about my own news, I just haven't had the chance until now.

"Charlie, are you…feeling okay about me having a baby? I mean…before you do?"

I bite my lip, half dreading her answer. It's not like we ever discussed there being some kind of pecking order with regard to Abbott babies, but I can't dispel the nagging guilt I feel every time I catch Charlie gazing wistfully at my belly. My big sister always talked about having kids—way before I ever, ever considered the possibility for myself.

She doesn't answer for a moment, and I'm starting to feel anxious for bringing it up at all when she finally says, "It hurt...at first. I was happy for you, but it hurt. I had a few bad days, honestly, just feeling like...it wasn't fair."

"I'm sorry," I say quietly.

"Don't be." Charlie turns a little to look at me. Her eyes are red, but she forces a smile. "I realized pretty quick that I can't be upset about something so good. And I'm really, really excited for you. That's the truth. I can't wait."

"You're going to be the best aunt," I tell her. "Livvie too. This is one lucky little bean."

"You're damn right," Charlie agrees, swiping at her eyes.

Gently, I ask, "Have you and Clayton talked any more about...those fertility treatments? I know the success rates are going up all the time."

She'd mentioned it to me at one point last year—and had been resolute about finding the best specialists and narrowing down the most effective treatments—but then she'd stopped talking about it. I hadn't wanted to press, but now my curiosity is getting the better of me.

My sister smiles sadly. "Speaking of mamas, we should Facetime Livvie and make sure she's not going crazy being cooped up with Miriam."

"Good idea," I say. I don't mention the change of subject as I pull out my phone and dial our little sister. "You think you'll keep calling her 'Miriam' forever?"

Charlie shrugs. "After all this time, 'Mom' feels weird to me. We'll see how it goes."

"Hi!' Livvie waves excitedly when she picks up the call and holds up a large bubble glass with a fancy stem. "Look, we're having margaritas!"

"*Virgin* margaritas." Mom's head pops into the corner of the screen. "I can't let her have too much fun, can I?"

They're sitting outside on a patio. The Louisiana sun is bright and appears to already have cast highlights in Livvie's hair.

"We're having a blast," Livvie says. "I wish you two were here!" She takes a long drink from a bright pink straw. "Last night, we had *alligator*."

Charlie and I look at each other. "That sounds like an adventure," Charlie says.

"It tastes like chicken!" Livvie spouts.

Mom adds, "I told her it was chicken so she'd try it."

"She did. She told me it was chicken." Livvie laughs. "It's a little chewier though."

"Ew," Charlie and I say in unison.

Mom and Livvie clink their glasses together—I'm

floored that they're getting along so famously, but I love it. We chat for a few more minutes and I let Livvie say hello to the horses and coo at them before we hang up.

On the ride back, Charlie gives me all the details about the New Year's bash she's organizing for the winery. It's going to be a challenge to top Livvie's headless horsewoman ride at Halloween, but I know we'll come up with something.

At the stables, brushing down our horses after the ride, Charlie suddenly says, "You know what we should do? Go on a babymoon! Some time away, just the two of us. I've always wanted to paint a sunset in Montana—maybe we can spend a weekend at one of the hot springs hotels that has a spa. It'll be a nice little pampering."

"Sounds like heaven. I'm in."

I don't remind her that we're both under watch 24/7 and it's highly unlikely that our spouses will let us go anywhere. But then again, maybe this will all get settled soon and Charlie and I can have our mini vacay after all.

We part ways after handing the horses over to the stable hand and I head into the house to take a shower before lunch. My inner thighs are sore from riding and my shoulders feel tense, although these minor aches are nothing like the one that's been plaguing my lower back for the past few days. Remarkably, the ride seemed to have eased that.

I'm just about to go upstairs when Dante comes down the hallway toward me, presumably on his way out, but he pulls up short when he sees me.

"You went horseback riding?" he asks incredulously, gesturing at my clothes.

I look down at myself, then at him. "Yes?"

"What the hell were you thinking? It's dangerous." His tone sharpens, as if he's two seconds away from giving me a serious ass chewing.

"Seriously? Women have been riding horses while pregnant for centuries. Eons, probably. And I'm still in my first trimester, Dante. It's fine."

I grab the banister, but he steps closer.

"No. It's not fine. No more riding, you hear me?"

Narrowing my eyes, I tell him, "Ytse is unflappable, and I'm more than experienced. We walked the entire time. You're overreacting."

He's shaking his head, refusing to listen to reason. "If you don't promise to stop riding, I'll sell every horse on the property by tomorrow."

Oh, that's it. "Are you done being a damn dictator yet?"

"I am not being a—"

Pulling off my riding gloves, I smack him in the chest with them. "Fine. How about we get a medical professional's opinion at my appointment this afternoon?"

"Yes! He's going to say it's a bad idea."

"*She's* going to say that moderate exercise is fine, even into the third trimest—"

"NOT on the back of a wild animal!" Dante spreads his hands as if I'm an idiot.

"DONOVAN!" I yell, startling Dante with my volume.

My driver appears, remarkably fast from wherever he'd been posting. He's never far away anymore.

"Get the car ready, please," I tell him. "I need a hamburger. And please, do stuff as many burly men into the car as you think I need to go to In-N-Out without getting murdered."

Forgetting about the shower and change of clothes, I follow Donovan out the front door, my riding boots clipping an echoing quickstep of rage across the marble floor.

Leaning back into the foyer, I call out, "See you at the doctor's at two, my dearest love," with as much sarcasm as I can muster.

Then I slam the front door behind me.

18

DANTE

As I watch the Escalade pull away with my brat of a wife in it, I have to remind myself that I probably can't handcuff her to a radiator in the basement. Probably.

Never mind that we don't actually have a basement. This is California, after all. But we do have cellars, a lot of them...and I'm sure she'd be fine wedged between a couple barrels of aging wine. At this point, I'll do whatever it takes to keep her safe. Not just from outside sources, but apparently also from herself.

I don't understand why she won't take this threat seriously, especially after what happened with her little sister. Frankie just stood in front of me joking about being murdered. What will it take to make her understand that none of this is a joke? She has no idea how many people are gunning for her—and worse, neither do I. That's what scares me.

Still fuming, I head to the dining room. My brothers are already there, both looking stoic.

"Francesca will not be joining us for lunch today," I tell them as I take my seat.

Marco raises his eyebrows but says nothing. Taking out my phone, I check to see if she's texted. Of course she hasn't. Which makes me worry. I don't care that she's with Donovan. I can't stop thinking the worst is going to happen.

"I suggest we take advantage of the opportunity to talk shop," I add.

Marco nods, Armani just grunts. His lips are pressed together in the way they are when he's irritated or thinking about a problem. I never like it when he wears that expression.

"I know that look. Whatever it is, spill it," I demand.

Armani looks up, then returns his focus to the tablet in front of him. "Which part?"

Fuck. "All of it. Start wherever you want."

An assistant from the kitchen appears and sets a plate in front of me—lemon pasta, broccoli rabe, some kind of fish in white wine with capers—and I take two quick bites to get something in my stomach before I lose my appetite.

"The Friscos are happy with their books," Armani says.

I swallow a sip of wine. "Good."

"So happy," he goes on, "that they've asked me to set up a new book for the spring baseball training camps. A less-often tapped market, but still lucrative enough for them to ask me for help. And they are asking rather...*heavily*."

Holding my fork above my plate, I stare at my brother. "Fuck the Friscos. You're not a bookie."

"I am now, it seems," he says dryly. "I'll keep you apprised of the situation."

"Copy that." I take a few more bites. "What else? Marco—you heard from Bryant?"

Marco shrugs. "Jim's pretty confident the tattooed guy is no longer in Napa. He's most likely been tipped off. We're increasing the search radius."

I grunt in response. We figured the guy had probably skipped town, but I'd held out hope for some sort of lead. Unfortunately, every bit of information Bryant has been able to turn up has resulted in a dead end. This tattooed asshole is some sort of ghost.

Considering the size and type of tatt on his neck, you'd think he'd be fairly recognizable. Which means a hell of a lot of people are covering for him. He must be a big shot in the underground to be able to pull this kind of disappearing act. That, or he's wanted by so many that he's learned to master the art of vanishing.

Marco gestures at Armani with a slice of garlic bread. "Tell Dante what you heard from the Chicago fam."

Armani sets his tablet aside, and I brace myself for bad news. We didn't make any official deals with our Chicago connections at the restaurant the other night—I hadn't lied to Frankie when I told her that—but we'd laid out our needs in terms of protective muscle from them, and in turn they had left us hanging on what the cost would be for lending a hand.

Now, it seems, they're ready to offer terms.

"They need to wash a few million in cash." Armani's cold eyes flick to mine. His mask is in place, hiding what he's really feeling. "They're willing to contribute the manpower if we help them out."

"There are a few people around town who still owe us a favor, or three," Marco cuts in. "We could get it done."

I let out a slow breath. Honestly, I'd imagined the price would be worse. Though I'd much rather just pay them in dollars and be done with the whole thing.

"They won't accept actual cash from us?" I ask.

"We, uh..." Marco folds his arms on the edge of the table and glances at Armani.

Armani clears his throat and cautiously says, "We don't have enough in personal cash reserves to meet their price. The number is high enough that our only option would be to take funds from the winery."

"No. We're not taking from the business." I shake my head.

"Agreed," Armani says. "But washing a few mill is going to be hard to do under the radar. We've got the winery to think of. We can't afford bad press, rumors, or speculation without damaging the Bellanti name."

"Pretty sure Dad already accomplished that," Marco points out.

Armani tosses his napkin on the table. "And we've done a hell of a lot to reverse it. Yet here we are again."

We go quiet, a brooding silence falling over the table, and I think about how deeply unsettled I've been since the dinner party the other night. I couldn't be at ease around the Chicago family. They're old school, by the books—there's no leeway in how they do business—and it was obvious at dinner that they were observing us to determine how easy we'd be to maneuver. They know we're vulnerable, so it's a perfect time for them to pounce. Maybe my unease with them is more than just concern over how hard they can be to deal with.

"Do we even know for sure it's not Chicago behind the whole fucking thing to begin with?" I muse. "How do we know the tattooed man isn't on their payroll?"

Armani frowns. "Farman has been solid in doing his research. He's turned up nothing that would connect them to Dad's accident or Marco's car. Reasonably sure it's not them, but..."

"Is Farman digging deep enough? You know how the mob buries things." Sitting back in my chair, I rest my knuckles on my chin. "We're going into this blind, and you're asking me to take Farman's word for it. We barely know the guy."

"That's what we hired him for, Dante," Armani says, exasperated. "At some point, we have to let him do his job so we can take the next step. This is it."

"Damn." My frustration gets the better of me, and I slam my fist down on the table, sloshing wine out of my glass.

Pushing back my tendency to overthink everything, I make a fast decision. We have to protect our family. It's worth any price.

I scrub my hands over my face and then look hard at my brothers. "Okay then. Just the cash. One last favor. That's it."

Marco's eyes widen. "But what about the business—"

"Are we getting out or are we diving back in?" I say, cutting him off. "We grew up mired in a world of shit and lies and unspeakable things because of Dad. I don't want my kid to go through that. Hell, I don't want the two of you to go through it anymore. I keep seeing those fucking posters around town and it just…"

Missing posters, with Bregman's face on them. Bregman, whose life Armani snuffed out in order to protect Marco. Bregman might not have been a good man, but even still, he had a girlfriend, a mother… people who cared. We did what we had to do, there's no question about it, but it wouldn't have been necessary if our father hadn't been tangled up in the kind of shit he was. Which is why, after this payoff, we're done.

"Okay." Marco nods slowly. "We're getting out, then."

"Out," Armani agrees. "We'll give them the cash. That's it."

We take some time to eat, to process what we all just agreed to do and the implications it will have for the winery, our finances, the business decisions we'll have to make going forward.

Looking at my youngest brother, my pulse picks

up and something clicks inside my head. He's the baby, isn't he? The one I used to piggyback around the vineyard. The one who always looked up to me and Armani, tagging along on whatever we did and driving us nuts. He never went anywhere without a toy car in each hand, right up until middle school damn near.

Racing is in his blood.

And he's *my* blood. I can't let anything happen to him while he's doing what he loves—or ever.

"How'd the race go in Vegas?" I ask him. "First time on the pro circuit, right?"

Marco's head snaps up at my question. He looks stunned that I care enough to ask. "Ah, good. We came in third, in a race that some people thought we might not even finish."

"Some people, huh?" I say.

"We showed them. And no shady characters popped up, either. Well, no more than the usual ones, of course." His voice lightens.

"Congratulations." Armani raises his wineglass. "I assumed you'd lost, considering that you didn't bring any women home with you to 'celebrate,' or whatever you're calling your weird sex stuff now."

Marco shrugs. "I mean, I would have, but there wasn't enough room in the cab of the truck with my huge...trophy."

It's a lame joke, but it's enough to break the tension in the room. We all laugh and it feels like a weight has come off a little bit. It's good to see my brothers' good-natured bickering.

"I somehow doubt your trophy is as huge as you think it is," I say.

"Look man, when you've got a huge one, you use it to your advantage," Marco says.

Armani rolls his eyes. "Which you didn't, considering that you came home alone. You see, there's a difference between size and skill, brother."

Marco spreads his hands. "I got size *and* skill, bro. Size *and* skill."

On that note, I get up and excuse myself.

As I walk out the door, Marco calls after me, "At least we know you're not shooting blanks, Dante."

"Fucking right, I'm not," I call back.

And I'm inordinately pleased about it, too.

19

DANTE

It's almost comical to see my wife's burly bodyguards sipping fast food milkshakes out of palm tree-printed paper cups with their sunglasses on.

As I pull into the doctor's office parking lot, I can see one of them leaning against the hood of the Escalade, and another posted at the front door of the clinic pretending to talk to someone on his phone. They're not exactly subtle, but that's fine. I don't want them to be. I want anyone who might be watching to know that my wife is protected.

Inside the waiting room, I spot Donovan's hulking form next to Frankie, a battered paperback held up to his face. His eyes dart to me as I walk in, then go back to his pulp novel. My wife doesn't acknowledge my presence when I sit beside her, though Donovan moves a few chairs away to give us a little privacy.

"Did you enjoy your burger?" I ask quietly.

"I enjoyed three." She picks up her own palm tree cup and slurps pink strawberry shake through the straw. "And I only puked up the first two."

She returns to the magazine spread open across her thighs, ignoring me again. The waiting room is small and there's only one other couple here. The husband eyes Donovan and moves a little closer to his very pregnant wife, who is scrolling on her phone. I wonder if he's nervous because of my bodyguard, or because of the impending birth of his child. And the myriad things that could go wrong. My gut knots and I shift in my seat.

The walls are covered in framed posters illustrating the various stages of pregnancy. Another depicts a woman discreetly breastfeeding. There's a series of black and white photographs of a woman giving birth, her bottom half covered with a drape. Can't get too graphic, I guess, or every man who set foot in here would bolt.

After an eternity of sitting in silence, a nurse with a clipboard comes out and says, "Francesca? You can come back now."

Frankie stands, and I do too, but she shoos me back to my seat.

"Sit down. I don't want you going back there."

"I thought—"

"Just wait here with Donovan," she says, gliding away.

I drop back down in the chair, a little stung that she doesn't want me in there, but also a little relieved I won't be going back to see all the instruments and needles and...things. I glance back over at Donovan. Still reading. I should have brought a book, too.

The minutes tick by while I look around the room. Up at the ceiling. Make awkward eye contact with the other man across the waiting room. Why is this taking so long?

What if something is wrong?

Frankie told me to be here, and I was. Hell, I was early. I should be back there with her. I should be doing...something. Shouldn't I? It's my kid, too, for fuck's sake.

The longer I sit, the more pissed off I get. Restless, I finally stand up—planning to march myself to the exam room and demand to hold a chart or something—but before I take two steps, the same nurse who took Frankie away opens the door and pops her head into the waiting area.

"Mr. Bellanti?"

"Yes?"

"The preliminary exam is done, so you can come on back. Right this way."

Relieved, I follow her into the hall.

"How'd it all turn out?" I ask anxiously. "Is it all...normal?"

She just smiles. "Dr. Shirvani will have details for you, and she can answer any questions you have. But since your wife's blood draw is finished, it's time for the sonogram."

Sonogram? My heart jumps in my chest. I'm suddenly more excited than I ever thought possible. I'm about to see my kid for the first time.

We enter the room to find Frankie lying on a padded table, her belly exposed. There's a slight bump there that I've noticed, but she's been wearing fall layers that keep it hidden—so this is the first full-on, daylight look I'm getting at it. I can't help staring at it, fascinated. There's a baby in there. Our baby. Growing bigger and stronger every single day.

Frankie reaches out her hand, looking slightly scared. I go to her side immediately.

"I'm still mad at you," she whispers. "But I didn't want you to miss this."

Dr. Shirvani comes in just then, all smiles as she greets me, shakes my hand, and then quickly gets down to business. Once there's a thick layer of gel on

Frankie's abdomen, the doctor puts the wand just below her belly button and starts slowly moving it around.

"Look!" Frankie points to the screen.

And...oh my God. "I see a head. And hands."

"Yes. And right there, those are the feet," the doctor says. "You can also see the heartbeat, but it won't be audible for another few weeks."

Frankie's hand is tight on mine. I stare at the screen in awe, as if I'm taking in a star-studded night sky full of unknowable galaxies. My vision blurs, making me blink a few times.

"Would you like to know the sex?" The doctor looks between us. "Technically, it's just an anatomical determination."

I panic, looking to my wife for help. She looks a little panicky, too.

"Damn that stone face of yours," she says. "Do you want to know or not?"

I'm not prepared to make this call, but I reflexively shake my head no.

Frankie smiles. "Okay. Me neither. But Dr. Shirvani, can you tell me what your thoughts are on horseback riding while pregnant?"

"In the first trimester, it's generally fine, as long as it's not vigorous and you're experienced. Moderate exercise is good for you and the baby."

"Ha!" Frankie says.

"But," Shirvani goes on, "there's definitely more risk on a horse than, say, riding a bike. Or going running. And since you are going into your second trimester, I'd weigh the risks seriously before continuing to ride. I wouldn't recommend it at all in your third."

I stop myself from blurting "ha" right back at my wife. But ooh, do I want to.

Dr. Shirvani looks at the monitor again, eyes scanning the screen.

"Everything's okay, right?" Frankie asks, sounding worried. "I didn't...hurt it, did I?"

"All good," the doctor says with a smile, turning back to us. "I was just checking all the boxes. Looking good. Here, I'll print a few photos for you to take. I love these new machines."

A row of somewhat blurry black and white images of the sonogram roll out, and the doctor rips them off and hands them to me. I've never seen anything so beautiful.

Frankie lets out a deep sigh of relief as the doctor finishes with the scan and wipes the gel from Frankie's belly. She's still clinging to my hand. I gently let go of her and carefully tear one of the images off the strip, then hand the rest to her as I slide the picture into my breast pocket.

In the car on the way home, with Donovan driving and the security team following in my car, Frankie takes my hand again and turns to me.

"Okay. So maybe trail riding is a little too much for the future..." she admits. "But honestly, that ride fixed my back pain like nothing else has."

I frown. "I didn't realize you were in pain. I'm sorry. I could've—"

"It's not that bad. I think it's just like, all my organs shifting around. I get this dull ache sometimes, shooting down my leg, like a nerve is twisted or pinched or something."

"Sciatica," I tell her. "Sounds like it."

"Well whatever it is, it disappeared after I got on Ytse. Something about the way the saddle moves my hips around, I don't know. But it made the ache go away."

I start thinking of all the things we could try. "I'll bring in a masseuse, an acupuncturist. Whatever you need to be pain free."

Frankie laughs. "Oh, there's going to be pain, Dante. Pain and swelling and cravings and all kinds of uncomfortable things. If there's one thing I learned from Charlie, it's that being pregnant is extremely gross sometimes."

"I didn't know Charlie and Clayton had a baby."

Her smile drops and she looks away, out the window. "They, um...didn't. She's had two miscarriages. And until today, I didn't even think about that happening to me. But now it's all I can think about."

I pull her against me, smoothing her hair back as she rests her head on my shoulder.

"I was born two months premature," she says quietly. "Growing up, whenever my dad got mad at me for doing something stupid, he'd say it was because I didn't cook long enough."

"Frankie—"

"I know it's not true, he's just an asshole...but what if something bad happens? What if I do the wrong thing, or not enough of the right things, or the baby—"

I cut her off with a kiss. "We'll buy every baby book we can get our hands on."

"How about just the good ones?" she says with a laugh.

"The best ones. I promise," I tell her seriously. "And when we get home, I'll give you a massage. I'm sure I can find a way to make you forget all those aches and pains."

"I'll take that bet," she purrs.

A lump forms in my throat and I hold her more tightly. "I swear to you, Francesca. You will be safe.

You are protected, both of you, and this baby is going to be perfect just like you."

"More perfect, I hope."

"That's not possible."

Frankie smacks me with a playful hand, her smile widening even further. "Look at you, flirting shamelessly with me. Sir, you have already put a ring on it and knocked me up. I'm not going anywhere."

I kiss her forehead and can't stop myself from reminding her, "You left once before."

Shit. I sound like an asshole. And I definitely didn't mean to sound so emotional about it, either. Frankie just stares at me, her hand loosening in mine.

"I didn't leave you, Dante. You drove me away. There's a difference between being safe and protected, and being in a cage. Being controlled. Being kept in the dark."

Her hand leaves mine completely as she looks out the window. I don't have a good rebuttal, but I steel myself to ask the one question that's been bothering me most since I collected her in Miami.

"Would you have come back if you weren't pregnant?"

Silence pulses between us.

Still refusing to meet my gaze, she says, "I'm here now, and this kid is on the way."

"But—Frankie, I love you."

She smiles sadly. "Sometimes love isn't enough."

"What more is there?"

Finally, she looks over at me again. "There's trust. Communication. *Choice.* A whole host of things. Compromising from time to time, even. But the biggest thing is trust. You don't trust me. Yet you've set this marriage up so that I have no choice but to trust you. How is that fair? How is that ever going to be…livable for me?"

I don't know what to say as her words tumble in my mind. She's right. But if I tell her the truth, tell her everything, it will change the way she sees me, feels about me. Irrevocably.

"I've seen the posters around town," she adds. "Of Bregman. I know he's missing. And I know that… that I'm the reason why he's probably dead."

My jaw goes tight. "He signed his death notice the moment he fucked with my father's car."

And I won't apologize for that, even if it makes me sick to think about what happened to him for doing it.

"So he is dead, then," Frankie murmurs.

Contemplating, I look at her, hesitating as I try to decide what to say—something, anything besides the truth. But she wants the truth, and my trust. I really have no choice.

"…yes," I answer.

Her face goes blank and then she turns back to the window, shrouded in silence. I watch her, wondering what she's thinking as we make the turn into the drive of Bellanti Vineyards.

And I make up my mind.

20

FRANKIE

Without a word, Dante pulls my chair back from the dinner table and takes my hand, pulling me to my feet.

I guess this means no dessert.

His brothers look at us conspicuously, but no one says a thing as we exit the dining room and take a left down the hall. My curiosity is piqued, but I don't ask any questions—I'm still pissed about the "talk" we had in the car earlier. The talk where I laid out exactly what was bothering me and he just sat there and said nothing. Nothing about trusting me or granting me personal freedom or even simply understanding where I was coming from. Asshole.

He turns into a doorway and I realize he's led me to the library.

"Sit," Dante says as he pulls out a chair facing a

heavy mahogany desk. There are stacks of papers spread neatly across the desktop.

I don't sit. "What is this?"

"I'll get to that in a second. Please, just sit."

Rolling my eyes, I comply.

Sensing this is more than a conversational chat, I look around the room. I've been in here before, of course, but I've never paid much attention to the details. Leather-bound books are arranged in perfect rows on gleaming bookcases against the walls. The furniture looks expensive but showroom new, as if it barely gets used, the air a bit stuffy as if the windows are rarely opened to let in a breeze.

"Just another pretentious room, isn't it?" I say. "Have you even read any of these books?"

He sits down behind the desk. "Most of them aren't real. They're just for show."

"Just like everything else in this house."

He smooths his tie and leans back. "You really don't like the house, do you?"

I shrug. "It's a beautiful. And huge. And cold and pretentious. Perfect for this cold and pretentious family."

"So you're not happy with the house."

"What did you bring me in here for, Dante? My ankles are swelling again."

With a sigh, he pushes the papers toward me. "This is everything you want to know."

My mood grows serious as I start to sift through documents filled with accounting, contracts, photos of random people along with short, typed reports like a private investigator might do. Copies of emails and bank statements and lists of names.

"When our father died, my brothers and I swore we were getting out of the mob. All of our loose ends were tied up, except a few betting books that the Frisco family was happy to take off our hands. We didn't owe anyone a single damn thing. That created the unheard of opportunity to get out, and we took it. We were finally clean. Ready to go legit. So we did.

"But then we found Bregman and...we got some more information."

"About your dad's accident."

Dante nods. "That wasn't all. He'd gotten paid to off Marco the same way, in a car accident. Bregman had plans to tamper with the race car. So we stopped him."

"You killed him," I say quietly, understanding dawning on me. "Neutralized a threat."

I search my husband's gaze, but all I see in his eyes are the familiar walls he keeps up.

"The threat didn't stop there, Frankie," he says quietly. "They targeted your sister, and if we didn't take immediate action, they'd have already come after you. Probably Charlie, too. Anyone close to the Bellanti family is at risk."

"Hence the security detail. And you being even more of a control freak than usual." I take a deep breath, absorbing it all. The pieces are clicking into place. "So what now?"

"We had to get back in," Dante says. "For the sake of keeping our family alive. We had no choice, not knowing who to trust or where the next blow might land."

Closing my eyes against his words, I set the papers on my lap. "You're back in the mob."

"For now, yes. We're working on an...arrangement of sorts."

A tingle races over my scalp. "Will there...will there be another chance to get out?"

His silence gives me the answer.

"Okay," I breathe. I take a moment. Then another. My eyes open. "Okay then."

His chin tips up. "Okay? That's it? That's all you have to say?"

I lean back in the chair. "Okay, I understand now. I believe you. And I'm going to take Donovan *everywhere* I go that isn't Bellanti property. Which will not be often."

"You're going to follow the rules, just like that?"

"Just like that. This is scary shit. The kind of shit that's forcing me to reframe everything that's happened over the last few weeks. I didn't know any of this before—but now I do."

He doesn't say anything for a second, just looks at me. "Well okay then."

"I mean, not quite 'okay then,'" I huff. "I'm still pissed that you kept all this from me and I'm not at all happy to find out that we're tangled up with the mob, but...I guess I'm more relieved that you've finally decided to trust me with all this."

Dante slips from his chair and gets down on one knee next to me. The warmth of his hand connects us as he slides his fingers through mine. "You can't tell anyone about this. Not your sisters, not your mother. No one. If you need to talk about it, you talk to me."

"I understand."

His eyes narrow. "Really? It's that easy?"

Slipping my hands around the back of his neck, I pull him closer. "Good things happen when you trust me, Dante. You keep forgetting that."

Taking my chin in his hand, he pulls me in for a gentle kiss.

"I think I'm starting to remember."

When he kisses me deeper, I slide my hands around the back of his neck and pull him closer. Dante scoops me out of the chair and holds me tight.

Pressed to him. Suddenly, he lets go and steps back, looking at my middle like something terrible just happened.

"The—did I squeeze you too hard? Did I hurt the—"

I touch his cheek, laughing. "You felt the bump? It's okay. You won't hurt the baby."

His brows knit together. "What about your back? How does your back feel?"

"Horny," I blurt.

He barks out a laugh. "Is that so?"

"It is. And I'm not going to break from a few kisses. But this is really serious, Dante. I might die if you don't take me upstairs right now and fuck me senseless."

That gets another laugh out of him, but I keep my serious face on.

"I have a very serious medical condition which requires intense physical therapy. And special medicine. Maybe even—"

"No. Frankie. Don't say it."

"—an injection," I finish.

I laugh as he shakes his head, then swoops me up in his arms, more gently this time. "That's it," he says warningly. "You're going to get it for that horrible joke."

"I can make up some more if it'll help."

He kisses me and carries me down the hall, then up the staircase. When we get to our room, he lays me on the bed and then steps back, eyes roving my body.

"Time to put your trust to the test." His eyes gleam.

"Oh *really*." My heart lurches excitedly.

He strips my blouse off, and then my bra. My nipples perk at the cool rush of air. Instead of tossing my shirt onto the floor like he usually does, Dante twists it into a rope.

"Put your hands against the headboard."

I do as he asks and he binds my wrists to one of the carved wood bedposts with my shirt.

"Comfortable?" he asks.

"Very," I purr. I'm antsy with anticipation. We've never had *this* kind of fun before.

His eyes never leave me as he works his tie free and then unbuttons his shirt. I revel in the view as he strips the shirt off, slowly revealing every hard dip and rise of his perfect abdomen and chest. His biceps bulge as he slides the tie between his hands and brings it toward me. I pull in a breath as he covers my eyes with the soft fabric and ties it snugly behind my head.

"Be a good girl and stay here," he says. "Don't wander off."

"Yes, master," I say teasingly.

I feel his body weight leave the bed. Moments pass, and my eagerness only builds, my insides getting hotter by the second. My slim skirt feels overly restrictive now, considering my top half is bare. Toeing off my shoes, I realize how gently my wrists are actually bound. I could easily slip out of this if I wanted to.

But I don't want to. I want to know what's coming next.

Dante finally returns, and I hear his footfalls cross the bedroom floor. He sets something down on the bedside table, and I hear the rustling of clothing as if he's finishing undressing.

Finally, his weight presses into the mattress next to me.

"Do you know how fucking hot it was to think of you up here," he says, his voice a low growl in my ear, "bare breasted and tied up, just waiting for me to make you scream?"

"I—"

Suddenly, something ice cold presses against my nipple, and I shriek.

"Fuck, that's cold!"

"Ice usually is," Dante says, but before I can say anything else, his hot mouth closes over my nipple, warming it back up.

"Ahh, that's good," I gasp. "I forgive you."

Dante swirls the cube around my taut flesh again. This time I'm ready, and I let out a quiet hiss. He teases me some more, alternating between cold ice and hot mouth, working me back and forth, again and again, until it's impossible for me to lie still. The dual sensations muddle my mind and I start begging for more.

"Good girl," he says. "You're mine, aren't you?"

He puts the ice in his mouth and sucks my nipples, tonguing me roughly as he does.

"*Fuck*. Fuck yes," I pant, writhing in my bonds, back arching up from the bed.

Each new wave of pleasure seems brighter, sweeter. His hands move over my body, my nerves super sensitive, every touch amplified. I've never felt anything so frustrating, but so good.

Finally, Dante rips my skirt off, slides my underwear down, and spreads my legs. Then he pushes into me, thrusting fast and hard, still working his cold-hot mouth over my breasts. His cock fills me so completely that I feel like I'm losing my mind.

"You're mine. Mine!"

"Yes," I murmur, my eyes squeezed shut beneath the blindfold. "Yes, yes, yes."

I'm so turned on already, I know it won't be long before I explode.

"Mine," he says, over and over again.

Dante rides me to the cusp and then pulls back, slowing his pace each time my moans get too close together. I push my hips up, seeking more. He spears into me deep and then holds still, fully sheathed, taking my chin in his hand.

"Come for me, Frankie. Come now."

At his words, I do. I feel myself shattering, clenching helplessly around his cock, my orgasm like a dam bursting, shivering as the shockwaves roll through me.

"Again," he says, starting to thrust again, hard and fast, fucking me relentlessly until I can't stop myself from climaxing a second time.

I'm gasping as I ride out the pleasure, so sweet it's almost painful, until I can't tolerate much more. But it feels so good…so, so good.

"One more time," Dante says.

"I can't," I admit, still breathless. "It's too much. I just need a minute."

"Shh," he soothes. "I've got something for you."

Dante pulls out and moves, the hot tip of his cock bobbing against my lips. Opening for him, I suck him down as he pushes into my mouth, fucking my throat in short, quick strokes.

"Swallow it," he commands. "All of it."

"*Mm-hmm,*" I moan around my mouthful of thick cock.

He explodes down the back of my throat and I drink him down willingly, my body trembling with adrenaline and pleasure. Suddenly, the blindfold comes off and the soft lights assault my eyes. Squinting, I peer up at my husband.

He's panting, a slow grin crossing his face. I know what he's going to say.

"Oh no. Don't say it—"

"You'll need to repeat your treatment at least once a week. Doctor's orders."

I groan, pulling my hands out of the loose knot and shoving him in the chest. Laughing, Dante takes me in his arms and rolls over the bed with me.

"Turns out," he says, kissing my temple, "good things happen when you trust me, too."

21

FRANKIE

The winter holidays are fast approaching, and Bellanti Vineyards is booming. It feels like not a day passes where we're not filling massive amounts of orders, shipping wine all over the world for all sorts of upcoming celebrations. Not to mention what's going on inside the offices. We're swamped, every single one of us, and it's only going to get busier.

Luckily, my morning sickness is finally starting to ebb. I can go entire days now without getting sick, though I do still get queasy at times. Thank God for my mom's tummy tea.

I'm in my office with Candi sitting across from me, a leather portfolio open on her lap. She's taking notes for our meeting the old-fashioned way, with paper and pen, something I appreciate—it feels more personal than having her eyes glued to a laptop screen. Both of us are chatting away excitedly about expanding the winery's distribution network, ideally further into South America and even Australia by next year.

"If we can just get someone in Antarctica to sell our wine, we'd be on every continent," I tell her. "Wouldn't that be incredible?"

"I'll start working on that for you," Candi says. "It'll be a fun market to break into, and a new challenge for me. I'm always up for a challenge."

"Excellent," I say, rubbing my hands together like a cartoon villain. "Expanding our reach is critical for our master plan."

"Of world domination?"

I laugh. "I like the sound of that."

She scribbles a few more notes while telling me about her contact in Sydney. "So I'll touch base with him tomorrow and get the ball rolling."

Candi taps the end of her pen against her lower lip. She's dressed in a lovely light blue suit with a ruffled-hem pencil skirt. The color brings out the golden highlights in her hair, which is gathered into a loose bun. She's wearing black framed glasses, too, and the effect gives her an all-around sexy businesswoman vibe. I wonder if the ensemble is for Armani's benefit, and if he's seen her today...

We're still going over all the paperwork when my

office door flies open and Dante storms in, his stoniest face in place.

"Can I help you?" I say peevishly.

Dante glares at Candi. "Get out."

His tone has me jumping straight up out of my chair. "*Excuse me?* You will *not* speak to my colleagues like that. And we're in the middle of finalizing a deal."

"I don't care," he says. "Whatever the deal is, it's off. Candi, you're done here."

My jaw drops. Candi starts packing up her things.

I cross my arms over my chest, livid. "You can't do this. I'm the VP of Operations."

"And I'm the fucking CEO," Dante shoots back.

"See you later, Frankie," Candi says, not bothering to say anything to my asshole husband before she hustles out the door, closing it behind her.

"What the hell is the meaning of all this?" I ask.

"You lied to me. You paid me lip service and then you went behind my back and did whatever the hell you wanted anyway." His eyes burn into mine and I swear I see red.

Fucking *what*? "I don't know what you're talking about."

Dante smirks cruelly. "The babymoon?"

My face flushes hot as I suddenly remember the

conversation I had with Charlie. I'd thought we'd just been daydreaming, making plans that *might* work out at some point in the future, maybe, but not ones we'd actually follow through with.

"Shit," is all I can muster.

"Yeah. Clayton just filled me in on your little plan to sneak off to Montana with your sister. You're willing to risk your life and that of our baby for a *fucking spa weekend?*"

I rub my temples, shaking my head. "No, Dante. It wasn't like that—it was just idle conversation. We were daydreaming. I wasn't planning on actually going. And I certainly never agreed that it would be—"

"Does your sister know that?"

I flip my hands palm up. "I *assumed* she did. I can't speak for her—"

"You're just trying to placate me so I'll let my guard down. You'll sneak away the second I turn my back. I can't believe you want me to trust you when this is how you act."

"You're impossible!" I throw my hands up. "And you're jumping to conclusions. I'm not going to stand here trying to defend myself when I've done nothing wrong. This conversation is over. I need to go try to salvage the deal you just ruined."

"I said the deal was off, so it's off," Dante says, doubling down.

"Get bent, Bellanti," I fume, stomping out the door.

I hurry to the parking lot, relieved to find Candi's car still there. Bending slightly as I approach, I look in the window. She's sitting behind the wheel, staring straight ahead. She's not quite crying, but it looks like she's on the edge of it.

I tap on her window. She jumps and then forces a smile. When I point to the passenger side, she unlocks the door.

Sliding into the car, I take a breath to settle my emotions. "Candi, I am so sorry about that. If it was up to me, this deal would absolutely be done already, but I'll have to work on him a bit, get things back on track."

Candi nods, waving me off. "I get it. It's fine. I just...really needed this deal. God, they're such assholes sometimes. The whole lot of them."

I can't argue with that. "You're not wrong."

She subtly blots the corners of her eye. Has business not been good lately? I know her reputation is flawless, and she used to be so busy that she was closed to new clients. But I don't feel comfortable prying. We're friends, but not close ones. There's still a boundary between us.

"Maybe you could talk to Armani and—"

"Ha. I don't think so." She looks over at me, her voice bitter. "He won't do a damned thing without Dante's permission. Trust me."

We're not going to get anywhere with this until I bring Dante around. Leaning over, I give Candi a hug and promise to work on my husband and call her next week with an update. It's too much money to be turning down just because of a tantrum.

I get out of the car and watch Candi leave, giving her a little wave as she rounds the curve in the drive and heads to the main road.

Pulling out my phone, I dial Charlie as I head back to the office.

"Hey, Frankie."

"So Dante just ruined your babymoon surprise, thanks to your husband's mouth."

"Awww." Charlie makes an apologetic sound. "I'm so sorry. Clayton's such a little gossip. He'll be sleeping on the couch tonight."

I laugh. I hope my sister can't tell it's a little forced.

"It's really okay," I tell her. "It's actually probably for the best. The OBGYN said it wasn't a good idea for me to travel long distances, so we'll have to raincheck it anyway."

I am purposely not mentioning Dante's shit fit

from earlier, because I don't need to give my big sister any more reasons to think my husband isn't treating me right. And since Charlie has no idea what's going on with the Bellantis and the unknown threat, his reaction will just seem overblown and controlling.

"Oh, um, yeah. We can totally raincheck," Charlie says, but I can hear the disappointment in her voice. "I understand."

"Sorry. But I promise, we'll go away and do something really fun as soon as we can."

"Yeah, sounds great. Unless..." There's a pause. "Okay, how about this? Meet me at the tennis court at seven tonight. Bring your favorite bathrobe. Oh, and make sure you come hungry. Now that you can actually eat without tossing everything right back up."

My sister sounds so chipper, and I want to say yes, but I need to make sure we'll be safe.

"We won't be leaving the winery, right?" I ask. "I kinda want to stay on the property."

"Not a problem—we won't go far. And this time I won't tell Clayton, so he can't ruin it. It'll just be me and you, on Bellanti property, having ourselves a secret girls' night."

I nearly agree, but hesitate again. My nerves are overwhelming me. But if we stay on the grounds, the guards won't be far away. What's the worst that could happen?

"Okay," I relent. "See you at the tennis court at seven."

"Yay!"

We hang up and I enter the lobby of the Bellanti offices. It feels chillier in here than before. Probably because I'm immensely irritated with my husband and the chill is following me around. I say hi to Ruby when I see her in the break room and then make my way to Dante's office, but he's not there when I peek inside. The light is off, his laptop gone. The scent of his cologne doesn't linger in the hall. Wherever her went, he went a while ago.

Fine then.

I'm not in a hurry for another fight. It's one step forward, eight steps back with him. Besides, if I can avoid him until it's time to meet my sister, then he won't have a chance to ruin it.

He's already ruined enough of my day.

22

FRANKIE

Dante comes down the stairs and finds me sulking in the living room, sipping tea and binge-watching *The Queen's Gambit* again. I know what he wants, but he's not going to get it.

"Dinner's ready," he says dispassionately. "We're already late."

"I'm going to skip tonight," I tell him, keeping my eyes glued to the screen.

"That's a terrible idea."

"Tell that to my stomach," I snap. "I don't feel like throwing up roast beef and baby reds, thanks."

I take the opportunity to slurp my tea loudly, but he doesn't budge from the doorway.

"I thought you'd been feeling better," he says.

Side-eyeing him, I say, "It's hit or miss. Some days are better than others."

That's not completely an untruth. His posture seems to relax a little.

"I can have some broth and crackers brought to the table for you," he suggests. "You should at least eat something."

"No. I'm going to lie down."

With that, I click off the TV and walk past him to the stairs. On my way up, I see him turn into the dining room without another word. Just as well.

In our room, I pack a small bag and then write a note to leave on the desk for Dante. It says I'm going out for a little while and that I'll be FINE. I also promise to be back before midnight. He'll be pissed, I'm certain, but hopefully he won't worry too much.

I kill some time on social media, scrolling mindlessly until I'm confident that dinner has been fully served—and that my husband and his brothers are occupied with their meals—before quietly sneaking out of the house. I navigate easily to the never-used tennis court, guided by the soft lighting scattered around the property. Charlie is waiting with one of the vineyard's UTVs on the other side of the chain-link fence. She gives a hushed squeal when she spies me coming.

"Hop in. Let's go."

I slip into the seat beside my sister, buckling up. "Where exactly are we going?"

"On a grand trip...to our old house. Which, before you protest, very squarely lies within the bounds of the newly expanded winery borders now, and therefore meets your demands."

She raises a brow at me.

"Or we can just hang out at the guesthouse—your call," she adds. "I don't want to make you uncomfortable or get you in trouble with the himbo."

Taking a second, I mull it over. The house *is* technically Bellanti property, but the lines are a bit sketchy. I don't know if the guards patrol that far, or if there's any protective oversight. And I should probably let someone know where I'm going—Donovan, at least—but I feel the spirit of rebellion welling up inside me.

Fuck it. I'm going to be impulsive.

Besides, if this is rebellion, it's got to be the mildest, lamest rebellion ever.

"Let's do this," I say.

Charlie lets out a whoop of delight and we take off into the night, at a safe speed but one that has my stomach fluttering with excitement nonetheless.

My sister drives us down a hill and then rounds the property toward our childhood home. A few minutes later, she parks the UTV in our old driveway and we hop out. The house is dark and silent. Suddenly, I'm struck with apprehension.

"You don't think Dad's here, right?" I ask.

"I know for a fact he's not." She digs around in her pocket and then jangles a key in my face. "Front door key. Thank goodness it still worked."

"Wait, you've already been inside?"

She loops her arm through mine. "Oh, yeah. You'll see."

We step inside, and I see battery-powered candles lighting our way through the house. Sneaky of my sister to use the soft flickers for illumination instead of turning on the lights, which might attract attention from my husband or the security team.

Inside the master bedroom and bathroom, Charlie has set up a full-on spa experience for us. Fancy scented Diptyque candles, soft music, face and hair masks, and two baskets full of body products, nail polish, and skin creams. A mini buffet of chocolates, sugared fruit, artisanal cheese and crackers, and other assorted goodies is spread across the top of the dresser.

"This is amazing," I tell her, awed by the effort she went through. "I love it. I can't believe you put this together so fast."

"I'm an event planner. Duh."

She laughs and gives me a squeeze and then ducks into the bathroom, returning a second later wearing a fluffy pink robe with leopard trim—it's fussy and fabulous and it could give my lavender and marabou number a run for its money.

"Where's yours?" she asks.

"In my bag," I tell her. "I'll go put it on."

"We look fa-reaking amazing," she says once we're both decked out. "Let's spa it up!"

Our hair masks go on first, and then we fill small paper plates with treats to eat during the half hour it will take for the masks to set. The bedroom is so big that there's plenty of space for the upholstered vanity chair and faux fur ottoman Charlie dragged in from Livvie's room, so we sit on them and drink apple cider out of champagne flutes while we talk.

This is nice, just me and her and a load of snacks. I needed this more than I thought.

There's just been so much going on...and the constant stress of the danger that Dante *swears* I'm in keeps me in work mode from morning till night, just so I don't have to think about it. It's still hard to process the fact that I married into the mafia.

After we rinse the masks out of each other's hair and get started on another round of pampering, I take the opportunity to ask Charlie about something that's been nagging at me.

"What kind of bad things do you think Clayton has done?" I ask quietly as she's painting my nails. "And how do you...you know, deal with it?"

Charlie pauses mid-polish and lowers the bottle. She's quiet as she studies my face, and then finally says, "Why? Do you think Dante did something bad?"

I don't answer, but my silence is probably enough of an answer in itself.

Returning to my nails, she says, "Here's the thing, Frankie. It's not like the movies. These people don't just run around committing criminal acts for the fun of it...well, maybe some of them do. But I doubt those people last long, because nobody wants someone like that working for them. Anyway, the point is, sometimes bad things *have* to happen—to prevent worse things. I came to terms with that a long time ago. It's the only way I can live with it."

"All for the greater good?"

"Yeah." She glances at her phone. "Crap, I almost forgot! It's two hours later there." Dialing Livvie on FaceTime, she warns, "Don't touch anything. You'll smudge the polish."

"Family spa night!" Livvie shouts from the phone screen. Her hair is pulled back with a headband, her youthful skin gleaming, gold crescent-shaped gel pads stuck under her eyes even though I know for a fact that she doesn't have undereye bags. She squints at the screen. "You guys look like mimes!"

Charlie and I laugh.

"It's Australian pink clay!" Charlie says defensively. "It detoxifies and tightens without drying. We're going to look ten years younger."

"Oh, please. You're both perfect just as you are. And will you look at you two in your frilly robes," Mom exclaims, leaning into the frame. "You look like old-timey movie stars!"

We strike dramatic poses for her, and she raises a flute of champagne and then takes a sip. The conversation turns chaotic and lively. It warms my heart.

"How's the little baby bean?" Livvie peers closer to the camera as I try to show off my small bump.

"Letting me eat, finally," I say with a grateful sigh. "And making me pee. A lot."

Mom claps. "The tea is working then?"

"Like a miracle. *Thank you*," I say.

"Wonderful! I was worried baby Azetta was going to malnourish you," Mom says.

I give Charlie a quizzical side-eye.

"Azetta? Did you just come up with that, Miriam?" Charlie wrinkles her nose.

"Of course," Mom says. "It's a delightful name. Don't forget, I named the three of you and I did an excellent job of it."

Livvie cocks her head. "I was thinking more of

like a Panina or Regatta. Something strong and no-nonsense."

"Panina as in…panini? Like the sandwich?" I ask. "And isn't a regatta a boat race?"

"How about Tiramisu?" Charlie suggests. "Tira for short. So cute!"

"Yeah, real cute. Why not Olive Oil?" I say dryly.

"I think Olive is great!" Livvie shouts.

"Well," Mom cuts in, "I suppose if you insist on sticking with Italian, Flavia or Druscilla might be better? Or, wait. *Delfina Bellanti*. Say it with gusto, all of you."

"Del-fina Bell-anti!" Livvie says with a theatrical Italian accent, kissing her fingers.

Charlie follows suit in a low-toned, male voice.

I don't participate, though I'm happy to see Charlie chiming in with real glee.

"You're all losing your minds. I'll name my own kid, thanks. And it's *not* going to be Delfina Bellanti. What if it's a boy?" I pause. "Oh God, please don't tell me your boy names. I don't even want to know."

We all burst into laughter. Finally the banter calms down, and Livvie asks about how the horses are doing.

"They're just fine. Nothing to worry about. I took Ytse for a ride the other day," I say.

She pouts. "I'm jealous. I miss them so much. Though I have to admit...I do kind of love getting to sleep in and have a little fun without worrying about getting to the stables twice a day. I'm still working out though, so I'll be in top form when show season comes around again."

Mom rolls her eyes. "Don't let her fool you. She talked about trying to put a saddle on Miggy more than once."

"Who, me?" Livvie takes mock offense. "I mean, maybe. It was a passing thought."

We joke and make fun and act like overtired teenagers on a sugar high, and before we know it we're all saying our goodbyes and promising to talk again soon. It's bittersweet, my heart aching when my baby sister disappears from the screen, but we still have face masks to rinse off and chocolate-covered strawberries to eat.

Charlie's just put her phone away when she freezes for a second, tilting her head.

"What's wrong?" I ask.

She shakes her head. "Nothing. I thought I heard something, but I think it was just the wind. Anyway, let's get our masks rinsed off. Mine's getting a little itchy."

"You can go first," I say, gesturing at the plate of cheese in my lap.

"Sweet." Charlie turns up the soothing music for me and then goes into the bathroom.

A few minutes later she pops back out, her skin looking dewy and fresh.

"Your turn," she says. "I left a towel out for you on the sink. It's a little messy. Try to use cold water, otherwise it kinda melts on."

"Thanks."

Just as I'm finishing rinsing my face, I hear Charlie's voice from the other room, but it's muffled by the door and the running water.

"What'd you say?" I ask, still patting my face with the towel as I exit the bathroom.

I stop dead in my tracks.

The towel drops from my hands.

Charlie is being held by two men, one of them with his huge hand over her mouth, her eyes wide with fear. My ears start ringing as every muscle in my body tightens, my flight instincts kicking in.

But before I can even think about running, another hulking figure lunges from the doorway, and the floor rushes up to meet my cheek with a hard crack.

I'm dazed at the impact, the wind knocked out of me.

My scream dies in my throat as the man's shadow falls over me.

23

FRANKIE

CHARLIE and I are tied up with torn bedsheets and made to sit on the floor against the bed while two of the men have a short conversation.

Black spots flash behind my eyes as a wave of dizziness washes over me. Charlie leans her shoulder against mine. Her breathing is rapid, yet soft, and I wish she'd say something so I could be comforted by her voice. But neither of us wants attention right now. Besides, the third man just came back trailing the sickening scent of gasoline, and I need to pay attention.

Gasoline gives us a cursory glance and then tells the others, "We're changing the plan."

"That wasn't the agreement," the shortest of the three says. "We burn it down to ash."

A small whimper escapes my throat, my pulse

pounding so hard I feel dizzy. As they continue to argue, it becomes obvious that they were sent here to set fire to the house—so that my piece of shit father can claim the insurance money. And from the sounds of it, there won't be anything left afterward. Our childhood home, and everything in it, will be destroyed.

Even worse: Charlie and I are now a liability. There weren't supposed to be any witnesses. I can feel my sister's body go taut as a wire next to me as the men bicker about what to do with us.

Gasoline finally grabs the smaller man by his coat collar and shoves him against the wall. "Don't you get it, asshole? We have the wives of two *very rich men* in our hands. We'll get a hell of a lot more from them than trying to burn down this shithole for the insurance."

"I'm in," the other man, who looks like a 'roided-up gym rat, agrees. "Insurance payout's gonna takes months, and if Abbott gets caught—if he's in jail—we don't get paid. But we ransom these bitches, we might just get the money we're owed after all. With interest."

He leers at both of us. It makes me think the "interest" he has in mind isn't monetary.

The other two men turn their eyes to us. Charlie trembles. I instinctively move to embrace her, but my wrists are bound behind my back and I can't move. Anger punches through the fear inside me. How dare these fuckers tie us up and talk about us like we're meat for the auction block?

"You have no idea who our husbands are, do you?" I say, glaring. "They don't make deals with petty criminals."

"*Frankie!*" Charlie whispers frantically. "Stop talking."

Gasoline bends down until we're face-to-face. He might have been handsome once, before decades of hard living and fights. Now he's just a goon with something dead in his gaze.

"I am petty," he tells me menacingly. "Petty as hell. And I know exactly who your husband is. He'll pay." He backs up and paces the room as he continues to talk. "And if I don't get what I'm owed? I'll get my payment another way. Maybe a few pounds of flesh."

Turning toward us again, he takes a gun out of his jacket pocket and sets it on the dresser with a heavy clunk. At the sight of the weapon, the blood drains from my face.

When he comes back over, he crouches down and slides a hand into my robe, groping my bare breast with a harsh squeeze.

I throw myself back, struggling to get away, but

he slaps me hard across the face. The violence reminds me all too much of my father. I cry out in fury as heat blooms in my cheek. Gasoline tugs open my robe, and this time I don't resist—but Charlie slams into him with her shoulder, desperate to stop him. It's enough to knock him off balance, but then he turns on her and punches her in the side of the head.

The sting on my face is nothing compared to the horror of seeing Charlie's body crumple to the carpet. She lands on her side, not moving.

"Charlie!"

Gasoline rakes a hand through my hair, grabbing a handful and using it to drag me to my feet, his grip so hard that my scalp almost screams. With my arms bound behind me, I lose my balance and stumble into an antique dressing table. The corner spears into my side, and I cry out at the shooting pain that goes through me. Maybe I've cracked a rib.

Unmoved, Gasoline wraps a hand around my upper arm and shoves me toward the other men. I drop to the floor before either of them catches me, my kneecaps taking the impact.

"Take them downstairs," Gasoline orders. "The house still has to be rid of any valuables before we light it up. And you"—he turns back to me—"you two don't act right, you'll burn with it."

Charlie moans. It's an awful yet beautiful sound. Thank God she's alive.

As we're dragged down the stairs by the short, stocky man and the musclebound thug, I start to feel a wave of nausea washing over me. My face goes hot and sweaty, and the familiar lower back pain I've been hit with lately suddenly comes back full force.

When they shove us to the floor in the living room, the throb in my side rips into a sharp, blazing slice that makes my stomach cramp so hard it takes my breath away. Wincing from the force of it, I clench my muscles in an attempt to hold the pain back, but it does nothing. A low moan comes out of me, nausea burning my throat.

"Shut up and don't fuckin' move," the gym rat says, and the two of them go back upstairs.

I'm in so much pain, I'm hyperventilating now.

"What is it?" Charlie asks, angling her body toward me. "Talk to me, Frankie. What hurts?"

My voice shakes as I tell her, "My stomach is... stabbing. And I have cramps. Like period cramps, but...more. Stronger."

Tears are streaming down my face, but Charlie shushes me. "It's okay. It's going to be okay."

"I feel like I'm going to pass out," I gasp through quiet sobs. "I think it's the baby. Something's wrong."

The look on my sister's face confirms my fear.

She's thinking it, too. And she would know all the signs of a miscarriage.

"You're not going to pass out," she says briskly. "Come on. Stay with me. Let's take some slow, deep breaths, okay?"

She inches her way over to me, gently resting her head against mine.

"With me, come on. Breathe in..." She pulls in a slow breath through her nose, holds it for a few seconds, and then lets it out of her mouth. "And out. In...and out."

I try to mimic her, but I'm crying too hard to be able to take very deep breaths.

"You're doing great," Charlie says, even though I know I'm not.

Heavy footfalls sound on the floor above us. Something crashes to the floor. The assholes are thumping around up there, trying to find anything of value to steal before the house goes up in flames. I hear glass breaking, and then something heavy comes toppling down the stairs.

Fresh tears wet my cheeks. This used to be my home. And as broken as it maybe was, it's still the place I grew up with my sisters. Where we learned to stick together and watch out for one another like we're doing right now. As much as I hate the man who calls himself our father, this house still means something to me, and it's killing me that intruders are smashing my childhood to pieces and stealing what they don't destroy. And if I lose the lima bean—

"I don't want to lose my baby," I murmur. "And I don't want to lose you."

"You won't. You're not losing anyone. They'll come for us; I know it."

Charlie is blinking back tears, too. We can't embrace. We can't do anything but bow our heads together.

"Do you still have your phone?" I hiss, suddenly remembering that I'd seen her tuck it into her robe after the FaceTime was over.

She shakes her head. "It's still upstairs. I left it on the bathroom counter."

"Fuck. How did they even get around winery security? That's the part I don't get. There are regular patrols around the whole property."

Charlie frowns. "Patrols? What the hell is going on?"

"Someone's been threatening the Bellantis," I admit. "Whoever took out Enzo tried to go after Marco next, but they got...intercepted first. I shouldn't be telling you any of this, but...we have a whole crew of mafia men stationed around Bellanti Vineyards and the Abbott compound 24/7. They're supposed to be protecting us."

"I never saw anyone here while I was setting up earlier," Charlie says. "You think it's a problem with shift changes, or is something else going on? This isn't adding up."

"I don't know," I say, my voice weakening as another cramp rips through me.

Urgent footfalls clomp down the stairs. My body stiffens in reaction, but the thug turns the other way, ignoring us. We're not making it out of this unharmed. I feel this in my bones. These men won't think twice about harming my baby or raping Charlie and me. And then they'll dump our bodies so we don't become liabilities. Even if they can figure out how to get away with ransoming us, they'll never actually turn us over in the end. We're dead.

Rain begins ticking on the roof, a branch slapping against the window. Another man comes flying down the stairs and into the living room. It's the smaller, stocky one. He grabs Charlie by the upper arm. She shrieks, then recoils as if expecting a slap. His hand is raised, but he doesn't let it fly.

"Tell me where all the good shit's hidden," he demands.

A hysterical laugh gurgles from my mouth as the combination of fear, shock, and rage comes to a head. "You think there's anything of value left in this house? Our old man sold anything worth the price of a beer."

Even his own daughter.

"You're lying," the man says. "A house like this? There's money in these walls."

"Look around! This place is falling apart. We used to have expensive paintings and furniture and family heirlooms, but they're long gone. Every wall has been stripped," I tell him, disgust seeping into my tone. "Hell, he even disconnected the original plumbing in the basement and sold it for the going price of copper. We didn't have running water for three months."

"There's nothing," Charlie adds quietly.

I'm about to tell the guy to let go of my sister and fuck off, but suddenly my stomach cramps again, a fresh well of pain flooding my abdomen and lower back. There's nothing I can do but moan in agony.

"Frankie!" my sister calls out, but her voice sounds far away.

Black spots dance in my vision as my entire body becomes a world of pain.

24

DANTE

I JUST FOUND Frankie's note.

I'd been so mad at her earlier for breaking her promise, and now I find the goddamned note she laid out on the desk for me.

Still, I'm glad she left it. As much as it annoys me that she's gone out without getting the okay, it's nice to know she didn't just disappear into thin air. And this isn't exactly unexpected—during dinner, I saw Donovan out in the driveway getting the Escalade ready for her, so I'd assumed she was planning another burger run. At least she's taking protection when she leaves the house. Donovan won't let anything bad happen to her.

Wandering onto my balcony, I realize a whole mess of dark, angry clouds have rolled in. There's a mineral scent on the air, a humidity to the breeze that portends a storm. I watch the clouds shift, feeling the first few light drops of rain pelting me.

Now that I've had some time to cool down, I feel a little bad about how I acted this afternoon, especially in front of Candi. Frankie really *had* seemed surprised about her sister planning the babymoon in Montana. But in the moment, I was too angry to reel my emotions in. Controlling my temper is still a work in progress, and all I could think of was Frankie's apparent betrayal. The way it seemed like she'd lied right to my face just so she could sneak off for a weekend with her sister. But I think I was wrong.

I think Frankie really *didn't* know about the plan. That even if Charlie had gotten the chance to spring the surprise, Frankie would have backed out with a polite excuse. She's worried about her safety—the safety of the baby—too. She wouldn't have gone. Unfortunately, once again, I yelled first and asked questions later. She didn't deserve that.

God, I fucked up.

A sudden gust of wind blows, spraying me with cold, hard rain. It's starting to come down stronger, so I go back inside and make sure all the windows are closed. Restless, I wander downstairs to the living room, where I find Armani watching football highlights on ESPN.

He's leaning back on the leather couch, a beer in

his hand. The sound of the sportscasters arguing blares from the television. He doesn't acknowledge me as I sit on the other end of the couch and try to relax. When the TV switches to commercials, Armani grabs the remote.

"Yo. You have to watch this play."

He rewinds the DVR, but I'm not focusing. My neck tingles. I roll my shoulder to brush it off. Something doesn't feel right. The restlessness—it's creeping all over me. Something's got me itchy, in a way I can't explain.

"Did you see that?" Armani settles back in his seat.

"Yeah."

"Pfft, you didn't even look at the screen."

I grunt noncommittally in response as I pull out my phone to check for messages from my wife. Nothing. Not that I blame her.

"Where's Frankie?" Armani asks. "She still feeling sick?"

Ignoring the question, I get up and head for the kitchen. "Want a beer?"

I don't wait for an answer; I'll grab him one anyway. His question nearly made me jump out of my skin. I don't know where the hell she is, but there's no way a burger run is taking this long, even if the line was backed up all the way down the street.

And now that it's raining, I can't stop a wave of nightmarish images of car crashes from assaulting me.

I have my phone in my hand and am just about to hit the call button when the crunch of tires on the driveway outside pulls my attention. It's Donovan, coming around the bend with Frankie's car. Thank God.

The tension inside eases some. She'll probably come sauntering in with a bag full of In-N-Out burgers and fries, slurping a strawberry shake in that obnoxious way she does just to annoy me. I swear, that woman has a hollow leg when it comes to fast food hamburgers. Or at least, she has since getting pregnant.

Returning to the living room, I hand my brother his beer and take a long drag from mine, waiting for the sound of my wife's steps echoing in the marble hallway. Eh, maybe the house *is* a tad ostentatious.

I put my eyes on the TV and sit, waiting.

And waiting.

Silence. Except for the rush of my pulse in my ears, which grows stronger with each second that I don't hear Frankie come in.

"Dammit." I burst from the sofa, ignoring Armani calling after me. Where the hell is she?

Running through the rain, I round the corner of the house and head to the garage, where I find

Donovan having a cigarette with another one of the hired security men. Donovan does a double take when he spies me dashing through the downpour.

"Mr. Bellanti?"

"Where's my wife?" I bark out.

Donovan flicks away the cigarette and stands. "I haven't seen her since this afternoon."

My scalp alights with painful pricks. "Didn't you just...take her to get dinner?"

"No, sir," he says, shaking his head. "I took the car to get an oil change from a buddy. He gives me a cheap rate after business hours."

Frantic, I feel a churning in my gut. "Fuck." Something is wrong. I knew it.

My phone rings. It's Clayton, Charlie's husband.

"Clayton," I say when I pick up.

"Yeah, I just got a tip—Papa Abbott's been spotted at a local motel. The Vintner. Oh, and is Charlie at your place? She said her trip with Frankie got called off, but she's still not home yet, and either her phone's dead or she isn't picking up."

"Frankie's missing, too. They must've snuck off on that trip anyway." I keep my tone in check, but inside, I'm fucking furious.

I can't believe Frankie skipped town after our fight earlier.

"I need to make some calls," I bark into the

phone. "Grab a few men you can trust and meet me at the motel."

After I hang up, I call Officer Bryant, telling him to put out an unofficial APB on the women and explaining what we know so far. "One more thing," I add. "Maybe it's best if Napa police stay out of the vicinity of the Vintner Motel tonight."

"Understood," Bryant says. "Talk soon."

Donovan's crestfallen expression fades as I turn to him, but not quickly enough that I don't catch it. I know what he's thinking. He failed in his job to protect my wife. All his years of loyalty are down the toilet.

Yes, I could think of it that way, but it wouldn't be fair to him. This isn't his fault.

"This isn't on you, my friend." I clap him on the shoulder. "But I do need you to help fix it."

"Of course. Anything."

"Call Farman and tell him to start getting together some manpower. We're gonna need to coordinate a raid on the motel."

Donovan's already got his phone out, scrolling through his contacts. "Yes, sir. On it."

That's when my own phone vibrates with a text from a blocked number. Huh.

I open the text, watching something download

slowly, and then a photo finally appears on my screen—and suddenly the whole world goes sideways.

"Jesus fucking Christ..."

It's a picture of Frankie and Charlie, tied up on the floor, a plain white wall behind them. Frankie has a look of fear and pain twisting her features, and Charlie's expression is one of worry. There's dried blood near Charlie's ear, and my wife's neck and cheek are blotchy and red, like someone has manhandled her.

"Boss?" Donovan says, his hand going to my shoulder.

I realize I've fallen to my knees on the concrete of the garage, the phone shaking in my unsteady hand. My temples pound, and my jaw aches from clenching it so hard.

A second text comes in: *Pay Abbott's debts or these two die after we're done with them. Painfully.*

If Abbott has my wife mixed up in some ransom gig...I'm going to fucking kill him. Hell, I might kill him anyway.

"Get the fucking car," I tell Donovan. "We roll. Now."

The Escalade squeals out of the garage as a steady stream of big black vehicles appear in my driveway. I throw open the door and climb in the back—seconds later, Armani bursts in and slides onto the seat next to me.

"Donovan filled me in," he says, slipping a gun into the back waistband of his pants.

We don't talk as we race to the motel. It's all I can do to keep my composure. My body thrums with pent-up rage and fear for my wife and child.

I see Clayton's group pulling into the lot just ahead of our contingent, black SUVs fanning out around the front of the motel. We fill in the spaces so no one can come in or out of this dump without being spotted by our brigade. When I get out of the car, Clayton is waiting for me, an automatic rifle in his hands and rage in his eyes.

"You get a text from a blocked number?" he says quietly.

I nod. "I don't know what the fuck is going on, but this motherfucker better talk."

He signs the number 12 and we take off across the parking lot, weapons at the ready as one of Clayton's men kicks in the door.

We burst in and surround Abbott, who's sprawled on the floor of the motel room with his face looking recently beaten, one eye swollen shut, a bloody scab formed over a gash in his temple. He's clutching a nearly empty handle of cheap rye and is trying to maneuver it to his mouth without sitting up.

Amber liquid sloshes over his face as we point our guns down at him.

"Where are Frankie and Charlie?" I demand, stepping one boot on his wrist so he has no choice but to let go of the bottle.

He laughs. Just once, and then again, longer and louder. "Lost your wives, eh?" He pushes himself up a few inches on one bloody arm. "For a bunch of big, tough men, sounds like you can't control your women very well."

Clayton lets loose a kick, square in Abbott's ribs, that has him choking and coughing.

"The fuck are they, Abbott?" Clayton roars. "Talk!"

"I don't know! I swear I don't know," Abbott says, finally realizing we're serious.

Clayton grabs him by the front of his filthy flannel shirt and launches him onto the bed. "All signs point to you, asshole. Where are they?"

Abbott falls back on the mattress. "I don't know! It wasn't me! That wasn't the plan."

This time, I grab him, punching him in his already-thrashed face with my fist. He sputters and spits blood, the smell of stale alcohol rolling off him as I get closer.

"What the fuck you two wailing on me for?" he says, dabbing at his split lip. "I said I don't know!"

I glower at him. "It's the least we owe you for the years of abuse and neglect you put your daughters through."

Clayton joins me, looming over Abbott with his gun displayed menacingly. "Charlie asked me to kill you, you know. And I do like to please my wife. So if you don't tell me where she is, I'm going to make her very, very happy."

"And I'm going to make sure it happens real slow," I add.

"Oh yeah," Clayton says. "Very slow."

Abbott swipes a rumpled sleeve over his mouth. "I don't know. Jesus Christ. How many times I gotta say it? You're asking the wrong person. I swear I don't know. It's the truth."

"I think you're a fuckin' liar," I say. "But I got a brother who's a genius with a pair of pliers, and I bet he can fix that."

Clayton pulls back, ready to strike again, but Marco's voice stops him.

"Wait! Someone else worked him over first," he says. "Who got rough with you, Abbott? Maybe that's who we should be looking for."

We step back and Abbott slides onto the edge of the bed, hunching over. Suddenly he looks a million years old, but I can't muster up any pity for the son of a bitch.

"Some of my creditors found me," he admits. "They roughed me up. Beat me until I agreed to an insurance scam."

"How? The winery isn't yours anymore," I say. "Didn't you tell them that?"

"The house is still mine," he says, looking up at me with defeat in his gaze. "It's insured for a lot of money. They're supposed to burn it down tonight. Then when I collect on the policy, they get it all."

Marco turns to Farman. "Didn't you say one of the UTVs wasn't turned back in to the vehicle pool yet?"

"Oh my God," I hear myself say. I look over at Clayton. "They never left the property. They went home."

And now Frankie and Charlie are tied up in a house that's about to be burned down. When all of our manpower is split, either here at the motel dealing with this bullshit, or following my orders to search for the women in town and at every airport and train depot within a fifty-mile radius of Napa, including Oakland and SFO. Motherfucking...fuck.

"We're not done here," I hiss into Abbott's face. "Not by a long shot."

I point to Farman. "They're at the Abbott house. Get over there. Take as many men as you can. And you." I turn back to Abbott. "We're not done here.

Not by a long shot. We'll be having a reckoning, and that's a promise."

Abbott shakes his head. "Ah, come on, Bellanti. We all got what we wanted in the end, didn't we? Don't be such a woman."

"My woman is twice the man you are, you sad sack of shit."

With one more punch—to his good eye—I take off, racing to my vehicle alongside Clayton and Armani, all the while praying that we aren't too late.

25

FRANKIE

"Still no response. This is bullshit!"

The men have gotten increasingly belligerent. The texts were sent to Dante and Clayton over an hour ago, but the thugs haven't gotten a reply yet. The tallest one—the one I've been calling Gasoline in my head—is the one who came up with this plan to begin with, and he keeps insisting that the ransom money is in the bag.

The thing is...I don't know about Clayton, but Dante's phone is practically glued to his hand. He should have responded by now. The fact that he hasn't is making me panic. I can't help thinking that something terrible has happened to him and Clayton, too.

Meanwhile, Charlie and I have been sitting here, tied up, listening to the three men haul anything that looked to be of value out of the house so they could load it into their truck.

One of the men found an abandoned bottle of cheap vodka my father somehow missed, and the trio has been passing it around for the past hour. Their voices have been getting angrier, their movements more impatient. Their expressions more leering and hungry when they look at Charlie and me. The smaller man and the gym rat are pacing the living room like caged animals.

Every time one of them walks by, I huddle tighter against my sister, the wall at our backs. The pain in my abdomen has abated, but my lower back still hurts and my stomach still burns with nausea.

The gym rat walks past us again, and then stops to trail a hand over Charlie's hair.

"Nice. Soft. Your man paid big money for this hair. I wonder what else he paid for?" He eyes her chest and trails one finger down the neckline of her robe. Charlie twists away, kicking out with her bound feet. The asshole laughs and tugs her hair until she stops fighting, then lets her go with enough force that her head snaps back.

"Quit messing around," the smaller man says. "We should probably move 'em, huh? We're still on Bellanti property."

"Fuck 'em," Gasoline says. "They have no idea

where we are, or they'd be here already. We're right under their fuckin' noses, with their wives to boot." He takes another swig of vodka.

"Besides," the gym rat adds, "if Bellanti does figure it out, we'll just shoot him when he gets here and make even more money. Let 'im fuckin' come! He's a dead man anyway."

"What's the price on his head?" the smaller man asks.

"I don't know the exact number. Gotta be at least a mil," the gym rat answers.

Dante was right. Someone *is* out for the Bellantis—someone with the money, power, and influence to put a hit out on them. The entire family must have a price on their heads.

Gasoline takes another long pull from the bottle and then looks at me and Charlie.

"I'm bored," he says. "How's about you two put on a show for us?"

He laughs, the others joining in.

"'How's about' *you* eat shit and die," Charlie shoots back.

The short, stocky perp is on her in an instant. "Hey, that's not very nice. Sounds like you need a lesson in hospitality."

He pulls her robe apart, exposing her bare breasts. The men whistle at the display.

"Stop it!" Forgetting my own pain, I launch from my curled sitting position and throw myself at the man, trying to get him away from Charlie.

Before I can do anything else, I'm grabbed from behind by Gasoline and yanked to my feet. Suddenly I'm lifted off the ground as he hefts me up and carries me into the next room, my dad's den. Charlie's voice cuts through me as she screams my name, the sounds of her own struggle making me desperate.

I kick and arch my back, twisting, jabbing with my elbows...anything I can do with my ankles and wrists bound. The man just laughs and forces me onto the floor. I land facedown on the carpet, my belly hitting the floor before I roll over. Pain blinds me, making me gasp.

I'm so stunned by it that I can't react as my robe is ripped open and hands track over my breasts and belly.

"Well, well, well," he says, his eyes tracking over me. "What do we have here? He knock you up already? Shame. I was gonna do it."

Groaning in agony, I twist away, but he pulls me right back. Distantly, I know what's happening—what's about to happen—but I'm so wrapped up in the pain banding around my belly that I can barely muster the awareness to even try to fight back. My whole abdomen is clenching. Squeezing. Setting me on fire. Draining the strength out of me.

He starts palming my breasts, slapping them and tweaking my nipples roughly. Tears streak down my face as I struggle weakly, but between the folds of my robe twisting around me and the fact that I'm tied up, I can't get away from him.

"Be nice, little lady. Maybe if you're real good, I'll take a few grand off your daddy's tab."

The cramping has started again, coming back full force.

"Please. I need a hospital," I pant, breathless with pain. "Something's wrong, please. The baby..."

Gasoline just laughs. "Fuck that. With the money I can get for killing a Bellanti, even a half-baked one, I might actually come out of this hole sitting real pretty."

Another wave of cramping—contractions, really —hits. And that's when I realize: the baby is coming, much too soon. I need a doctor.

"You fucking snake," I gasp through clenched teeth. "You bastard. You fucking—"

I'm cut off with a backhand across the face, hard enough to knock my head back, and then he starts kissing me, his disgusting mouth suffocating me, his rancid tongue against mine.

I jerk my head side to side, screaming, trying to

kick at him. But it's not enough. He's on top of me now, using his knee to wedge my legs apart, the pain in my body almost unbearable as he presses his full weight on me, scrabbling clumsily at his belt buckle with both hands. I squeeze my eyes shut and let the tears flow, feeling myself float away from the violence.

Suddenly his weight is lifted completely off me. Curling into a fetal position, I bring my shoulders around my head for some protection and lift my knees as high to my chest as I can. I'm gasping in pain, barely aware of what's happening. But the worst doesn't come.

Boots scuffle on the wood floor. Someone grunts, fabric ripping. The heavy slap of flesh hitting flesh, followed by a crack and a scream. Slowly, I open my eyes to look.

Dante is here. He has the Gasoline man by the front of his shirt and is raining punch after punch straight into the guy's face, driving him back against the wall as he beats the shit out of him. But hit after hit, Gasoline just laughs.

"It's just a matter of time, Bellanti. You're a dead man. You, your father. Your mother and sister. And now your kid. We'll get all of you in the end."

A chill races over me and I realize I'm mostly naked. I try to shift my body so the robe covers more of me, but the shooting pains make me stop and moan.

Dante glances down at me, catching the look in my eyes.

Without another word, he pulls out a gun and shoots the laughing man point blank in the face. The gunshot is loud, an acrid smell in the air, and I see the body drop to the floor almost in slow motion.

Shock rips my breath away, leaving nothing but a buzzing sound in my ears. I'm babbling out loud, telling Dante the baby is coming, but I can't seem to hear my own voice.

Or Dante's, for that matter.

Dante.

His eyes, full of worry. My robe pulled around me, wrapping me in warmth. I'm so cold. My hands are free, wrists and fingers numb. Dante takes my hand in his, but I can't feel his touch. I'm so, so cold.

"The baby—" I try to tell him, but he just kisses my forehead and gently gathers me against him.

Blood and violence are all around me but I focus on Dante, his scent. His warmth. His protection. I nuzzle my cheek against his chest. The pain is lessening, and the world seems to be fading away.

And then I fall into the darkness.

26

DANTE

"What's happening? What's wrong with my wife?"

In the back of the ambulance, Frankie's delicate hand is cold and limp in my grip. She's hooked up to a heart monitor and a blood pressure cuff, the soft *blip, blip, blip* of the monitor making my own blood pressure soar. The paramedics arrived fast, but they've been wearing grim expressions since first laying eyes on her and haven't said anything encouraging about her condition. She's been in and out of consciousness since they got her on the stretcher.

I've been willing her to live the whole time.

She won't open her eyes long enough to look at me. She won't answer any questions. Every now and then she comes to enough to realize she's in pain, and

I hear her moaning. But no matter how encouragingly I squeeze her hand, she doesn't squeeze back. Every time she knocks out again, I'm afraid she's dying.

The female paramedic performed an exam in the house before they wheeled Frankie out to the ambulance. I asked the medic what was going on, but she couldn't give me a straight answer. Not about Frankie and not about the baby. She said a doctor would know more. She also said they don't have a monitor in the ambulance to check the baby—so we have no way to really know how dire the situation is until we reach the hospital.

When we arrive, the ambulance backs into the bay outside the ER and a team rushes out to meet us. I'm still hanging onto her hand.

"You can let go now, sir. We've got her." A nurse reaches for my hand and gently encourages me to let go of Frankie. But I can't.

I can't let go.

"Sir," she says a bit more firmly. "You need to let go now so we can take her."

"No."

Because letting go might mean letting go forever. What if she and the baby don't pull through?

The paramedic looks into my eyes. "It's okay, Mr.

Bellanti. They're going to take good care of her. I promise."

I can't do it. My vision blurs, and my chest hitches.

The stretcher has been lowered on its wheels and the team is waiting outside the ambulance, ready to take her inside. They're all looking at me, trying to be patient. I know my wife needs to go with them. Yet I can't allow myself to be separated from her.

One of the medics says, "Mr. Bellanti, it's urgent that we get your wife into the ER so she and the baby can receive a more complete exam. I need you to let go now, or I'm going to have to call security."

"Nobody wants to call security, sir," the female paramedic says softly. "I promise I'll come get you as soon as the emergency room doctor is done looking her over."

They pull the stretcher away, detaching her fingers from mine, and then drop the wheels to the ground to roll Frankie out of the ambulance. I watch the team push her through a set of glass doors that slides open automatically and then closes again. My wife is gone.

After I climb out of the ambulance, I just stand there, frozen, feeling completely and utterly lost. Memory after memory of Frankie floods my mind.

The way she looked in her dress on Halloween. Her laughing with Greg on the sales floor. The light scent of sun that always clings to her hair. The way she made me feel when we made love on the beach. The way I'd laughed with her. Really, truly laughed.

The more I think back, the more I realize that I've never been fully myself until she came into my life. And now all of it—my wife, our happiness, our future, our child—might be taken away from me.

I'm not sure how much time passes before Clayton appears at my side, clapping me on the back with a masculine half-hug.

"Dante. One of the paramedics said you might be out here."

"Where's Charlie?" I ask.

"Inside. We followed the ambulance in Bryant's patrol car. She's mostly okay, but she's still waiting to be seen by a doctor and checked out in case she has a concussion. Bryant's in there with her."

Idly, I make a mental note to send the Napa PD and the EMS team very large crates of wine this Christmas. Then I realize Clayton's still talking.

"...said he's going to have to talk to them about the incident and take down their official statements for his report, but he's made it very clear to the detective that the two men were killed in self-defense during a home invasion. There won't be any charges, he says."

I shake my head. "Wait. Two men? There were three. Where'd—"

"Armani and Marco have him," Clayton says, lowering his voice. "He's in the Deep Cellar. Bryant doesn't know anything about there being a third, and he assured me he'd steer Napa PD in the right direction as far as the crime scene is concerned."

"Good man," I say.

"He also said if one of our wives mentions a third man in their statement...he'll go on record saying it's likely head trauma or PTSD. Officially, only two men were found at the scene. Any evidence will corroborate that."

So a very *big* crate of wine for Officer Bryant in particular, then. With a lot of green paper lining the box as well.

"It's gonna be okay," Clayton tells me. "The guy'll talk, name some names, we'll start connecting the dots. This'll all shake out."

I want to believe him, but the truth is, my fear and rage and panic in this moment has little to do with any outside threat to the Bellanti family—and everything to do with my wife being in an ER bed right now, her life and the life of our child hanging in the balance. I start to pace, setting off the sensor on the automatic doors and whipping my head to check if it's someone coming out here with news about Frankie. But of course it isn't.

"What the hell is taking so long? It's an *emergency* room. I thought they were supposed to move fast."

Clayton hesitates and then shrugs to himself. "I've been here, you know."

"I...heard something about that," I admit, stopping to look at him. In fact, Frankie had mentioned Charlie and Clayton losing several pregnancies.

He nods. "I don't know what's going on in there, and everything may be 100% okay—I hope they are. But if the worst does happen with the kid...you can get through it. Together."

I feel his hand bracing my shoulder, and for a second, I can almost hear my father's voice in my head: *Don't show any emotion. Don't show any weakness. Don't let anyone know what you're thinking or feeling.*

Shut the fuck up, Dad.

Reaching out, I put an answering hand on Clayton's shoulder, acknowledging the offer of support with a nod.

Just then, the ER doors slide open and we both look over. Charlie is being pushed out in a wheelchair, her face battered and bruised and steeped in sorrow. The nurse leaves her as we rush over, Clayton sweeping his wife out of the chair and up into his arms.

"What's going on with Frankie? What did they say?" I ask, frantic.

"Nothing," Charlie says, turning her face toward me. I can see her eyes glistening with tears. "I still don't know anything yet."

Sobs wrack her body and Clayton tucks her head under his chin, gently holding her.

My eyes fall to the bandages wrapped around Charlie's wrists. Frankie had marks there, too. Raw and almost bloody from her efforts to get out of her bindings.

Rage begins to tick in my brain. These women had fought for their lives. Frankie had been kicking and screaming at the man on top of her, and his hands had been all over her, touching her, pressing her down and—

"...Mr. Bellanti?"

I hear my name coming from far away. Clayton nudges me, drawing my attention to a nurse standing in front of us. She looks like she's been waiting for me to respond for some time.

My breath hitches in my throat and I struggle to swallow it down. "Yes?"

"You can see her now, Mr. Bellanti. She's asking for you."

My legs go weak. I hang onto Clayton's shoulder, and Charlie pulls me into a hug.

"She's—she's alive?" I ask over Charlie's head.

The nurse just smiles. "Come with me."

27

FRANKIE

In...and out. In...and out.

I pull another breath in through my nose and then let it out slowly through my mouth. I'm doing my best to concentrate on my breathing, trying to keep it steady, but it hasn't been going so well. Ever since I woke up in this hospital room, I've been shaking uncontrollably.

Not because I was surprised to find myself here. Even as I struggled to stay conscious in the ambulance, part of me was still aware enough to know what was happening to me and where I was being taken. The hospital itself isn't what's making me tremble.

It's the memories. The nightmare of what Charlie and I went through. My brain just keeps replaying all of it, down to the last detail, over and over again. The horror of being tied up and held captive. The feel of that man on top of me, the smell of gasoline and alcohol rolling off him. How utterly helpless I was, how it felt to see Charlie getting hit and touched and violated. The moment I realized there was nothing I could do, when the fight in me started to die.

And my baby...nobody has been able to tell me anything. They keep saying I have to wait for the doctor. So I've been riding the edge of a panic attack ever since I opened my eyes.

I look down at my shaking hands and turn them over. Some of my nails are broken, my fingers abraded. My wrists are bandaged but they still feel raw, and I can make out the shadow of dark blood under the gauze.

Footsteps sound down the hallway, and when I look up, I see the nice nurse I had earlier walking into the room—with Dante following behind her.

A flood of relief goes through me. I reach for Dante's hand, and the feel of his fingers in mine brings tears to my eyes. Suddenly I'm shaking again, but for a different reason.

"Hi," he says softly.

He clasps my hand and kisses my knuckles, his eyes searching mine. All I see in his gaze is worry, relief, love. This is what I need. This, and the truth about whatever is going on with the baby. Because I need to know. The not knowing is worse.

Just then a doctor in a long white coat comes in with a male nurse, who is pulling an ultrasound machine behind him.

"I'm Dr. Wyn," the doctor says. "I'm going to run your ultrasound in a second, once the nurse gets the machine all set up. I'll be right back."

Dante nods. "Thank you."

She smiles kindly and steps out.

As the nurse works on hooking up the ultrasound machine, Dante looks back at me. He must have so many questions, and I'm not sure I have all the answers. Where did the men come from? How did they know Charlie and I would be inside the house? Where the hell was the security team meant to keep the entire Bellanti property safe?

Dante pulls a chair right up next to the bed and sits, gathering me close so he can kiss my forehead. Leaning into him, I can't help wishing he could climb into the bed with me. The warmth and security of his body is all I want.

"How's Charlie?" My voice is scratchy and weak.

"Recovering. She's with Clayton. I don't have all the details, but it seems like her injuries boiled down to scrapes and bruises. No concussion."

"Thank God."

"They wanted to keep her overnight for observation, but she refused. Said she's going home. They've already discharged her."

I swallow hard. "Good."

The male nurse turns to me and says, "All ready for the ultrasound, Mrs. Bellanti."

Dante eyes him suspiciously. I don't blame him. I'm not even sure that I feel 100% secure having a man put his hands on me after what I've been through.

"I just need to lift the hospital gown over your belly," the nurse says, coming over to the bed.

"Okay." I brace myself as he gently pulls the white sheet down. But the second he starts to lift the hem of my gown, I flinch.

Immediately, he takes a step back. "Would you like to do it yourself, if that's more comfortable? I just need the abdomen exposed for the ultrasound wand."

Gratefully, I nod.

"Not a problem. I'll give you a moment," he says, crossing the room to busy himself with some settings on the machine.

Dante takes over where the nurse left off, carefully lifting my gown over my abdomen while making sure I'm still covered from the hips down with the sheet.

I notice he's staring at my belly, brows drawn together, and that's when I look down and realize I have a massive bruise on my side, black and purple and ugly. There's also a small, grazing cut near my belly button. I start to shake again. Dante's hand grasps mine and tightens.

"We're ready," he tells the nurse, his voice strained.

"Great. I'll go get the doctor. Be right back."

Moments later, he returns with Dr. Wyn, who moves with soothing, unhurried movements as she wheels the ultrasound machine next to my bed and takes a seat.

"I have some good news," Dr. Wyn says. "The CT scan of your brain came back clear, with no signs of head trauma."

As she goes on in more detail, all I can think about is the way that man grabbed me by the back of the head and slammed me facedown onto the floor. Getting dragged down the stairs, falling into the vanity table. I guess I should feel lucky my injuries weren't worse—but right now, all I feel is rage toward the men who did this to me and Charlie. Rage, yes, and the sheer panic of not knowing if my baby is safe. Which is something only the ultrasound will tell us for sure.

"...x-rays of your chest show several hairline fractures on the seventh to tenth ribs, which is likely the source of those shooting pains you felt in your abdomen," Dr. Wyn continues. "You also have severe external bruising over your ribs. That being said, the fractures will heal on their own in a month or two, so in the meantime you'll just have to take it easy. We can give you some mild pain medication for the discomfort, but taking into account your pregnancy, options are limited. The safest thing for you is going to be acetaminophen."

"So just Tylenol, basically," I say.

"That's right," she says.

Dante squeezes my hand gently. "But what about the contractions she had?" he asks.

Dr. Wyn nods. "So what you described, Mrs. Bellanti, are Braxton Hicks contractions—a kind of false labor. They're unfortunate but perfectly normal and most women do experience them during pregnancy. Think of it as the body's way of practicing for the birth."

"So...not early labor," I say with relief.

"You're certainly not in labor now," Dr. Wyn says with a gentle smile. "But we'll keep you here overnight just to be sure."

"Thank you," Dante says.

"Shall we move on to the ultrasound?" Dr. Wyn

says, motioning for the nurse to turn the lights off in the room.

Soft gray light spills from the ultrasound screen. Dr. Wyn readjusts my gown and then squirts ultrasound gel across my abdomen. How different it is this time. Instead of excitement and anticipation, all I feel is overwhelming worry and concern. Even knowing my contractions were probably nothing, I can't help fearing the worst.

As Dr. Wyn moves the wand over my belly, Dante tightens his grip around my shoulder. When the doctor turns the screen so she can see it better, my heart lurches to my throat. Dante leans forward, straining to see the screen.

"And...it looks like your daughter is perfectly healthy," Dr. Wyn says.

We both let out a breath of relief. And then I realize what the doctor just said.

I turn my head to look at Dante, and his eyes meet mine. An awed smile spreads across his face. *A daughter*, he mouths. I nod. My heart is so full, it feels like it might burst.

After the doctor leaves, the nurse informs me that I'm going to be transferred to a private room for the night. Dante excuses himself to go deliver the good baby news to Charlie and Clayton. The mild sedative Dr. Wyn gave me must kick in then, because the next thing I know, I'm coming to in a different room with pale blue walls, soft lighting, and a huge vase of flowers by the window. It's a struggle to keep my eyes open. My brain does not want to be awake.

"Hey, sleepyhead," Dante says from a chair by the bedside.

I reach for his hand, stifling a yawn. "I'm exhausted."

"Go back to sleep. I'll be here when you wake up," he says. "I'm not going anywhere."

Shaking my head, I look into his eyes and say, "I wanted to tell you something first."

"Okay."

"I'm sorry," I say.

"Frankie, don't—"

"I am, though. I don't know what I'd do if something had happened to the baby. I'd never forgive myself. I just...I really thought we would be safe on Bellanti property. I thought there were security guards all over the place. I never for a second thought —" my voice breaks.

Dante brushes back my hair, shushing me gently. "You *should* have been safe. Something went wrong. And I swear to God, whoever is responsible is going to pay."

I see his jaw clench, his shoulders tense—and I

can't help wondering how he intends to make the men responsible pay.

Charlie said to never ask. That it's just the way this life is. Mafia wives don't ask questions. But my sister and I and my baby were almost killed tonight because of who we're married to. Mafia wife or not, I deserve to know.

"Are they going to pay with their lives?" I ask softly.

Dante hesitates. He's not going to answer me, and I suppose that's answer enough. But then he rubs my arm. "Maybe. Let's not talk about it right now."

He doesn't want to upset me, I can tell.

But he doesn't know what I'm really thinking.

My eyes close, and I feel myself start to drift off again. But I can't yet. I need to tell him…something…important.

"That other man…at the house. I'm glad you shot him," I tell Dante groggily.

And then I slip into a deep, dreamless sleep.

28

FRANKIE

The vineyard's New Year's bash last month went off without a hitch, despite the fact that the entire Bellanti family was conspicuously absent from the festivities. I chalk the success up to a combination of my older sister's event-planning superpowers, and the hard work of the few loyal staff members who've been tasked with holding down the fort. Everyone else employed by Bellanti Vineyards is on paid furlough while the property is being renovated during the winter months.

The official story is that all of the Bellantis are spending time in Italy during the winery's renovations. Which is true...partially. The renovations *are* happening, but in reality, it's only Armani (and a trusted bodyguard) who went to Italy. Apparently, Armani has a real talent for blending in, so he's doing some digging into who wants the Bellantis dead, following up on the scant information obtained from the third would-be arsonist before he...decided to stop living.

Meanwhile, Marco is quietly touring all the prominent racetracks in the US, scouting for talent for his growing racing company. He started his journey by hand delivering Max to Livvie down in New Orleans and making sure she was settling in at the new safe house. She and our mother were recently relocated to a different property in a private, secure location known only to the Bellantis, since we don't know how deep the betrayal of our family goes. Armani made the arrangements. He chose a place that's up to the right standards for Livvie to resume her training with a vetted horse trainer, and under the watch of her personal bodyguard. She's finishing up high school with a private tutor, also heavily vetted. By all accounts, things are going well.

What else? Mom is painting again, a pastime that had fallen by the wayside over the years, now rekindled by her phone calls with Charlie. Sometimes they even paint together over FaceTime.

It seems like all our wounds are starting to heal...in more ways than just physical.

Now, making my way out the front door of the house and toward the Bellanti stables, I pull the collar of my wool coat tighter against the crisp February air. Morning sunlight spills down through dark gray clouds, but it offers little warmth. Once I reach the barn, I find the inside pleasantly cozy as I make my way down the aisle. For the past few weeks, I've been obsessively checking on our two very pregnant Friesians. They're due to drop their foals any day now, and their stomachs are huge.

"Hi, sweet girl," I say to Avina when she pops her head over her stall door in greeting.

She and Maeije both get an oatmeal treat from my pocket, along with a few nose pats. When Avina nuzzles me for another, I give in immediately. I know what it's like to have pregnancy cravings. And now that my morning sickness has mostly passed, I can't stop eating. Especially hamburgers. Speaking of which, I'd do just about anything for a hamburger right now. Fried in mustard, well done, with pickles. Mmm. This baby is definitely a carnivore.

At the sound of footsteps in the aisle, I turn around with a beat of alarm going through me. But all I see is Dante walking my way, a greasy paper bag in his hand, as if he has all the time in the world. The moment I see him, I relax. I wish the skittishness would stop. Hopefully, in time, it will. For now, I'm comforted by the fact that my husband rarely leaves my side.

"What's in the bag?" I ask, raising a brow.

"A snack," he answers, holding it out in offering.

The blessed man. I grin.

"Good answer." I snatch it out of his hand and excitedly peek inside.

The smell hits me right away: cinnamon, fried dough, sugar, maple. Hot, fresh donut holes. From the looks of it, two dozen of them. Mmm.

"They're from that place you like on Lincoln," Dante says.

"Thank you," I mumble around a mouthful.

Things between us aren't perfect, but we've found a nice rhythm to our relationship since I left the hospital. I feel like we finally have a solid foundation, one based on mutual trust and open communication. Dante includes me in his plans and takes my suggestions when they're workable, explaining things to me when they aren't. He actually listens when I stick to my guns about something. And he's learning that compromise doesn't mean an idea has to get diluted or weakened—that often, it can become even stronger.

"How's your back feeling today?" he asks, watching me scarf.

"Decent. And my ribs are good, too. Haven't felt so much as a twinge in like a week."

"That's exactly what I wanted to hear." He kisses

me on the tip of the nose. "Because, as it turns out, I have a little surprise for you."

"How little?" I ask teasingly. "Or are you going to tell me size doesn't matter?"

Just then, Avina and a few of the other horses perk their ears. I catch the faint *whump-whump* of helicopter blades in the near distance. The sound steadily comes closer.

My eyes widen. "Is that...?"

Dante grins. "I realized that you've been stuck hiding out at the winery for over a month now while we've been trying to consolidate resources and hire on more security. So, to give you a little break, I arranged a helicopter ride with Dean."

"Yes!" I clasp my hands together and practically jump up and down. I *have* been feeling pent up, and this is exactly the kind of excitement I've been craving.

Dante takes my hand and we head out of the stables and toward the helipad. When we reach the helicopter, Dean jumps out and gives me a high five.

"Hey! My best puke-aimer! You're a legend, man."

Dean's praise has me laughing. Dante looks less than amused.

"You, uh, you sure you're okay to do this?" Dante asks me. "We can reschedule..."

I narrow my eyes at him. "I should be fine. But I'll keep a bag close by just in case."

Throngs of excitement go through me as we ascend into the sky. We're high enough that I can see the freshly turned earth next to the vines where the hyssop and clover and other new secondary pollination crops will be planted in the spring. I can't wait.

Soon, I can also see the construction crew that's working on the old Abbott house. Dante had gained ownership of it from my father under...less than polite circumstances...but it meant that my father had no legal rights to anything near me or my sisters anymore. With the help of (and in partnership with) Delores Alvarez, Charlie is now in the process of turning the house into a bed-and-breakfast. She promised me that once the renovations were complete, no trace of our unhappy childhood would remain within those walls. She's also handling the remodeling of the old horse trainer's quarters in the Abbott stables—they'll soon be an updated apartment for Livvie to move into when she's able to come back to Napa. I honestly can't think of any other place my little sister would feel more at home.

As we whoosh over the property, I feel at peace just taking in all the muted tones of winter brown and gray below. In a handful of weeks, these hills and valleys will be alive with greenery and new life. I wrap my hands around my belly. There's going to be a lot of new life around here, soon.

My daydreaming is interrupted by Dante, who takes my hand and gestures out the window at the small, narrow valley on the Abbott property with the gorgeous view that I've always loved so much.

I gasp to see bulldozers down there, clearing the largest part of the land, taking out rocks and smoothing ridges and uprooting old oaks, though most of the trees are still intact. This valley offered so much solace to me as a child and teenager. What the hell is he doing to it?

I turn to him with a questioning frown, but before I can say anything, my headset crackles and I hear Dante say, "Welcome home."

What?

"That's where our new house will be built, Frankie. Brand-new, built to all of your specifications. You can make it as cold and pretentious as you want. Or not."

My jaw drops. How often did I daydream about living in a fairy-tale cottage in this very valley? A perfect escape, a place of tranquility with nature all around. And now it's happening. My daughter can have a warm and welcoming home, the home I always wanted for myself.

"There will be nary a marble floor or fake book in

sight," I tell Dante through the microphone on my headset. "The cycle of cruelty stops with us."

My tone is joking, but I mean every word.

"No more bad parenting," Dante agrees. "And no dark paneling or disapproving portraits of past ancestors either, right?"

"Well...maybe just a few disapproving portraits," I tease.

Leaning over, I give him the tightest hug and biggest kiss I can manage while pregnant, strapped into a helicopter seat, and wearing a headset.

Then I rest my head on Dante's shoulder, watching our little valley out his window as we slowly turn and fly away.

Dante runs his finger over my cheek. "Are you happy, Mrs. Bellanti?"

"Deliriously so, Mr. Bellanti."

Once we're back on the ground, we lean into each other as we watch Dean fly away, the wind from the helicopter blades tossing our hair.

"So. How was your helicopter ride?" Dante asks.

"Best ride ever," I say, turning to face him and wrapping my arms around his waist.

"Best life ever." He kisses me. "And it's only going to get better."

EPILOGUE

FRANKIE

"Livvie's going to love this one."

"What are you torturing her with now?" Dante asks, looking up from his laptop behind his desk.

"Paint samples for the new house," I say with a laugh. "She's going to hate every second of it. And I'm going to keep sending them to her until she helps me pick out a color."

Dante chuckles. "Cruel and unusual. You know she's just going to pick some random color to shut you up."

"Oh, I know. But it's still fun to tease her."

We're in his office at the Bellanti house, where I've settled myself on a couple pillows on the floor, a rainbow arc of design palettes and paint and fabric samples spread out before me.

I snap a high-angle selfie of the setup before

taking another big bite of one of Delores's spiced fruit cups. Then I text it to Livvie with a caption that says, "My heaven, your hell."

My baby sister notoriously hates anything that has to do with decorating—in fact, the closest thing I can imagine her having any design interest in is the layout of a horse stall. Sure enough, a second later, I get a vomiting emoji in response.

I return to my samples, mulling over shades of chalk paint in marine and French blue, muted tones that will make the living room a place of restfulness. Or do I want it to be more energetic? Bright whites with a few sunny yellow and poppy red accents? It's so hard to choose.

I'm interrupted by my phone chiming with another text from Livvie—this time, she's sent me a video. I wait for it to download and then press play.

Livvie's on a black horse that must be Max, and she's in a blue tank top with her golden hair pulled back. Seated behind her on the horse is her new bodyguard, tan and blond and shirtless. Although the picture is wobbly, thanks to Livvie's grip on the phone being jostled, it looks like they're riding through a pond. Both of them are laughing. I can see Miggy splashing along with them under the bright Louisiana sun. I watch the video again, studying this young man on the horse with Livvie. Her caption reads, "My heaven."

That's my sister's bodyguard? Holy hell.

Mom had mentioned what he looked like and had said that she thought there might be something going on between the two of them, but I hadn't expected...this. In Mom's opinion, the whole thing was charming and romantic, but she had supposedly cautioned Livvie against mixing safety with pleasure. She's only eighteen, after all.

Still.

I can't quite judge her. The dude is hot.

For a second, I think about showing Dante the picture, but then decide against it. I'm sure showing him hot dude pictures is the same brand of torture that I've put my sister through with the paint samples she couldn't care less about. It doesn't stop me from looking at the video again, though. This time, I hit pause and study Livvie's bodyguard more closely.

Beyond the male model good looks, he's tall—or at least, taller than Livvie is while sitting behind her on a horse. His eyes are light, a blue-green that almost matches my paint samples, and that tanned skin is pulled taut over some very well-developed chest and shoulder muscles. In fact, the only thing keeping him from looking like sheer perfection is the large black tattoo I can just make out that stretches over his pecs and up the side of his neck. I'm not the biggest fan of tattoos in general, though I admit it's an interesting design...it looks like a deer with huge antlers. Or maybe those are branches. I can't quite tell with the grainy quality of the video.

He has one possessive arm wrapped around Livvie's middle. Or maybe he's just holding on to her to keep his balance. There's no way Livvie would allow him on the back of her horse if he wasn't a decent rider and didn't have a moderate understanding of riding. Sexy body notwithstanding.

I better pass this video on to Charlie, so she doesn't miss the action. But first things first.

Sighing, I set down my phone. I have to use the bathroom. Again.

"Dante," I call out pathetically, raising my hands in the air like a helpless child. "Help."

He looks up from his laptop. "Again? What's it been, ten minutes?"

"Hey, you did this to me. It's only fair that we both suffer the consequences."

With a laugh, he gets up and comes around the desk, takes both my hands in his, and pulls me gently to my feet. "You're not allowed to use that line until you're in labor."

"No, no, no. I get to use that line any time I feel

like you deserve it. It's not my fault I have a bladder the size of a walnut right now."

Dante shakes his head. "How about this. You work at the table in the dining room, or I'll make room for you at my desk. If you sit in an actual chair, you won't have to keep getting up and down from the floor."

"It's much more fun this way, trust me."

Wrapping my arms around him, I kiss him on the cheek, utterly content.

And I can't help thinking...maybe Livvie will find contentment with her hot, blond bodyguard, too...

If you loved Dante and Frankie's story, be on the lookout for the next chapter in the Bellanti brothers saga...

Marco Bellanti falls for the one woman he shouldn't in the upcoming angsty, sizzling Forbidden Series.

Marco's story begins with Forbidden Bride.

PAIGE PRESS

Don't miss what's coming next from Paige Press!

The Billionaire and His Nanny

* a virgin nanny with a crush
* a brooding British single dad
* a bitchy ex wife
* secrets
* scandal
* an angsty road to happily ever after

Coming January 2022

Sign up for our newsletter so you won't miss this or any release from any of our authors.

ALSO BY STELLA GRAY

The Zoric Series

Arranged Series

The Deal

The Secret

The Choice

Convenience Series

The Sham

The Contract

The Ruin

The Convenience Series: Books 1-3

Charade Series

The Lie

The Act

The Truth

The Bellanti Brothers

Dante

Broken Bride

Broken Vow

Broken Trust

Marco

Forbidden Bride

ABOUT THE AUTHOR

Stella Gray is an emerging author of contemporary romance. When she is not writing, Stella loves to read, hike, knit and cuddle with her greyhound.

Made in the USA
Middletown, DE
09 September 2024

60051490R00177